Race to Glory

Samantha Alexander lives in Lincolnshire with her son, husband and a variety of animals including a thoroughbred horse, Bunny, and a pet goose called Bertie. Her schedule is almost as busy and exciting as her plots – she writes a number of columns for newspapers and magazines, is an agony aunt for teenagers on BBC Radio Leeds and in her spare time she regularly competes in dressage and showjumping events.

D0566617

Books by Samantha Alexander
available from Macmillan

WINNERS 4

Race to Glory

Samantha Alexander

MACMILLAN CHILDREN'S BOOKS

First published 2002 by Macmillan Children's Books
a division of Macmillan Publishers Limited
20 New Wharf Road, London N1 9RR
Basingstoke and Oxford

www.panmacmillan.com

Associated companies throughout the world

ISBN 0 330 48441 9

1 3 5 7 9 8 6 4 2

A CIP catalogue record for this book is available from
the British Library.

Phototypeset by Intype London Ltd
Printed and bound in Great Britain by
Mackays of Chatham plc, Kent

One

"Give me room!" I yelled, terror rising in my throat.

The other racehorse cannoned nearer, across the course. My horse Murphy's Law and I were being squeezed out, forced up against the jump wing, pushed off our line. It would end in disaster.

"What do you think you're doing?" I tried to scream. But the wind tore the words from my mouth before they even formed.

The other jockey swung closer. Stirrups clashed. I cursed. The shoulders of the two horses brushed together, pulled away, touched again. Murphy's ears snaked back. Up ahead, a five-foot birch fence drew closer. We were on a collision course. Nothing could save us. For a split second I saw the jockey's face. And then I knew. This was no accident. He meant it. He was deliberately riding to make us fall.

Fear paralyzed me from head to toe. I lost a stirrup. The third from last fence was about ten strides away now. About six seconds and counting. The wing of the jump was much higher than the fence, and set at an awkward angle. It was there to stop horses running out, to funnel them towards the correct take-off. We either had to stop dead in our tracks or haul to one side and bail out. But I was riding Murphy – the big, powerful chestnut who had never refused in his life. He wasn't a quitter – he'd burst his heart before slamming in his heels, and with sickening dread I felt him prepare for the leap ahead.

The rest of the field was behind us, labouring through the thick mud. The grandstand and finish were tucked in on a sharp right-hand bend, obscured from view by a conifer wood. We could have been in the middle of nowhere, for all the company we had. It was desolate. Just me and the other jockey, and the two horses. And he wasn't letting up.

"BACK OFF!" I screamed. I thought he might relent. I thought he might open up a gap, that he'd scared me enough. But no. He leaned forward over his horse's neck and drove into us harder, a menacing black silhouette with no regard for either horse's life.

Terror took on a new edge. I felt uncertainty ripple through Murphy seconds before he launched into the air. He corkscrewed pitifully, striving for height, but it was useless. It was asking the impossible. Time slowed and snagged as the horror unfolded.

His forelegs smacked hard into the brush. We somersaulted and torpedoed into the ground, nose first. Instinctively, like any professional jockey, I curled up tight to avoid injury. An extended arm or elbow would nearly always result in a break. My arms closed over my head as Murphy's great bulk slid along the drenched ground. Thirty seconds later, thirteen tired horses and jockeys took off over the top of us.

Shouting, slapping, a swish of birch, a horse squealing in panic, veering to one side. Then nothing, just the sound of hooves sucking out of the puddled track, and then they were gone.

But Murphy was still down. "Murphy!"

I was galvanized into action. His eyes were rolling into the back of his head. His flanks heaved, fighting for oxygen. His fiery red chestnut coat was daubed brown with mud and sweat. "Murphy!" I flung up the saddle flap and tugged at the girth.

An ambulance drew along the white rail with two Red Cross paramedics inside. A vet would be arriving any second. I knew what was wrong – he'd done it before – it was as if he gave so much in a race that when he fell there was nothing left to help him. He had to wait for life to filter back.

"He'll be all right, he will. He'll be fine. Come on, Murphy. Come on." The bitter wind cut straight through my thin silks until I was a shivering wreck, but I still instinctively threw my arms over Murphy protectively. If anything happened to him . . .

A roar went up from the grandstand just as a Range Rover spun to a sticky stop centimetres from the wing of the fence. "Justina!" A young man in a vivid red pom-pom hat leaped out clutching a lead rein and a feed bucket. It was Scooby, a good friend and one of the lads from our stables, Dolphin Barn.

"Where's the darned vet?" A gnarled older man followed him, stabbing at the ground with a stick. It was the Guv'nor, the man in charge of Dolphin Barn. Wretched with worry they both ducked under the rails towards us. It was like looking into the faces of two ghosts.

Aware of all the people around him who loved him most, Murphy suddenly snorted and lifted up his head. I pressed my fingers into the corners of my eyes and thanked God. He was all right. He swung his neck sideways and then staggered to his feet, stretching out one hindleg, then the other. He looked dazed, with a scratch over one eye, but unharmed. I was so weak with relief that faces blurred together. Suddenly I was aware of my own discomfort. My neck was sore. It felt as if it had

4

been clamped in a vice for twenty-four hours. It's said that if you hit the ground at a particular angle, you break your neck. I was beginning to believe it.

"What the devil did that squirt of a jockey do to you?" The Guv'nor was practically transmitting electricity he was so angry.

I knew that neither the guv'nor nor Scooby, who had led me up to the start of the race, would have been able to see what had happened from the paddock, from where they would have watched the race. It relied totally on a camera placed strategically alongside the jump to relay back the truth.

"Did Dougie win?" I needed to know, but it made my windpipe constrict just thinking about it. Dougie Barnes was a dirty rider who'd try any trick in the book to win, and he also detested female jockeys. He openly declared that girl jockeys shouldn't be allowed to race and should be sent back to muck out stables where they belonged. Not only had he robbed us of victory, but he'd frightened me on a racecourse for the first time in my life. Anything could have happened at that fence. I was lucky to be walking back alive.

Murphy strode out down the middle of the racecourse towing Scooby along at his side. Suddenly a great cheer broke out from the grandstand as the famous red horse came into sight. Crowds were going crazy with relief that he was OK. In the last six months, Murphy had become a celebrity racehorse. And I had become a celebrity, too. At sixteen and entered for the Grand National, I was being badgered to go on the radio and television, from Radio One to *Country File* and *Blue Peter*. My best friend, Mandy, had even set up a Murphy's Law fan club, selling pencil cases and T-shirts and school bags embellished with Murphy's proud head.

"I don't believe this," the guv'nor muttered. Suddenly there were more cameras and reporters on the racetrack than could ever have been around the winner's enclosure.

Murphy's long ears twitched as he basked in the attention.

"What's your reaction to the stewards' enquiry?" A forceful woman with a gravelly voice stuck a microphone under my nose while running backwards to keep up with us.

"He can't be allowed to get away with riding like that."

"Sorry? You do know that Dougie Barnes has lodged a complaint? He's saying that you rode into him deliberately at the fence before you fell."

"What?" I pulled up in amazement.

"Dougie Barnes," she raised her eyebrows at

my blank face. "He says this fall – it was all your fault. The stewards are looking into suspending you . . ."

Two

"Calm down, Justina," National Champion jockey Ben Le Sueur touched my arm as I burst into the weighing room. He was Mandy's boyfriend and I could see he was torn between the obligation to help and the urge not to get involved. He was also trying to speak to someone on a mobile phone. The weighing room was where jockeys congregate to get changed and to prepare mentally for the race ahead. It was a haven from the public and the media, and usually bubbled over with friendliness and good humour. Now, though, it felt like a morgue.

"Where is he?" I scoured the line of pegs for his set of colours. "Don't tell me he's still in the shower." Most of the jockeys were out in the paddock waiting for the next race.

Davido, an Italian jockey, came down the aisle dressed in just a pair of ladies' tights. Jockeys often wore them under their breeches to keep the cold out. After a year in communal weighing rooms, there were no surprises left. "Where's Barnes, Davido? I know he's not in the next race."

"The complaint's been dropped," Ben interrupted with some relief, turning off his phone. "It's been withdrawn because, coincidentally, the camera by the woodland fence has been blown down in the wind, or so the stewards say."

"More like deliberate sabotage by Barnes before the race, if you ask me," I muttered.

"You don't know that." Ben's voice was tight.

"I'd say it was pretty obvious."

A thought suddenly dropped like a stone into my brain. Why hadn't it come to me earlier? It had been raining during the race, yes, but visibility was good. The other jockeys hadn't been that far behind. The stewards didn't need photographic evidence, not if enough jockeys came forward to say that they had seen Barnes cheating. Ben's eyes slithered away from mine when I asked him.

"It was hard to see anything, the rain was driving into us, my goggles were steamed up. The other lads will say the same."

I gulped back shock and felt the muscles in my neck tighten with pain. Gingerly I eased myself down on to the changing-bench and let my head drop forward into my hands.

"You're all terrified of him, aren't you? You risk your lives without a second thought in this bone-crunching game, but along comes a has-been jockey from Country Kildare and you're scared of opening your mouth."

"You don't know."

"I know I'm a sixteen-year-old girl who he's just tried to kill, and that I've got more pluck than you lot put together."

"That's enough." Ben seized my wrist. "We're just wise enough not to go looking for trouble. That's the difference." He was pressing into the veins in my wrist. I looked down and he quickly let go, leaving a thumbprint on my skin. The tension was super-concentrated.

"I want to give you a word of advice. Don't antagonize Barnes. Just let it be, even show him some fake respect if you can manage it." He saw the sourness in my face. "I mean it, Justina, don't play with fire. Barnes is inhuman. He's ruthless and obsessive and he'd ride over his own granny to get what he wants. Stay well away."

Davido had disappeared. Even the valets who cleaned the saddles and organized the silks had vanished.

A drizzly rainbow arched over the racecourse as I went down the steps into the parade paddock. The rare sunshine did nothing to lift my mood. No jockey in the country was going to support my case against Dougie Barnes. That was painfully clear. There was one exception though, and my heart dipped just thinking about him. Rory

Calligan, my boyfriend, who had taught me to race ride and with whom I'd been madly in love for years. But I wasn't going to tell him what had happened. In fact, I was going to make sure he didn't know anything at all. I could stand on my own two feet without running to my boyfriend at the first sign of trouble.

The next race had just finished. A group of horses wrapped in a misty haze of sweat and hot breath clattered into the enclosure. There was a jubilant feeling as a steel-grey mare slotted into the winner's place and the jockey leapt off her back Frankie Dettori style. But I wasn't interested in watching the happy throng. I moved purposely past the secretary's office and the saddling stalls, and ducked under some ropes, heading in the direction of the stables.

I wanted to see Murphy. By now Scooby would be washing the mud out of his hooves, and sponging the caked sweat from around his girth. He'd chuck the bright green woollen rug over his quarters and lead him out for some grass. In an adjoining stable would be Gertie, Murphy's travelling companion, a small black-and-white goat who was devoted to her horsey friend, but loathed being told what to do by humans. Her favourite trick, which she usually reserved for the stewards, was butting people in the back of the knees.

It wasn't long before I was recognized. It was

inevitable, especially as my hair was dyed emerald green at the ends and I was still wearing my silk breeches. People turned and whispered and nodded. I still hadn't got used to it, being recognized all the time and pointed at. It made me feel awkward and sent the colour rushing to my cheeks.

"'Ere, luv," a woman with a Liverpool accent pressed a fifty pence coin into the palm of my hand, "that's for luck over the big fences. We think Murphy's the best thing on four legs since Pegasus."

I was awed by the number of people who came specially to see us race. The big red horse had touched so many hearts.

"*Racing News*," a man pushed forward. "Are you still going for the National? Was it true that you deliberately rode into Dougie Barnes?"

"Um, I'm in a rush, sorry. Can I speak to you later?" In a panic I dived forward, towards the car park where horseboxes are kept. I had to learn how to cope with the newspapers, I couldn't keep running away.

"Are you Justina Brooks?" A stable lad carrying a headcollar and rug stopped me.

"Who's asking?"

"Just passing on a message," he shrugged. "A bloke said could you meet him at the horsebox. Said his name was Scooby."

12

The Dolphin Barn horsebox was parked at the end of a line, immaculate with its burgundy colouring and black stripe, the same as my racing colours. I glanced up at the six square little windows even though I knew all the horses would be in the temporary stabling. Scooby must be in the living quarters. He must have forgotten something. There was no one else around.

I picked my way round the car park through long squelching grass. "Hello, Scooby?"

No answer. I took another step forward. And then someone grabbed hold of my left arm and jerked it so hard that the rest of my body spun round and I crashed into the side of the horsebox. The side of my head felt as if it had split in two. It was a few seconds before my vision steadied enough to see directly ahead. When I did, I wanted to be sick. Dougie Barnes was leering at me like a school bully in the playground, confident he could get away with it.

"Had enough yet?" He laughed with a hard edge.

"Oh, for God's sake," I peeled myself off the side of the horsebox trying not to show the terror that was leaking into my stomach like acid.

He thrust the muddy black-and-burgundy silk which had come off my skullcap into my chest. "Look what I kindly collected for you," he grinned. I knew I'd lost it out on the racecourse

13

when I fell and had intended going to collect it later.

Dougie Barnes leaned close, with one hand over my shoulder resting on the box. I could see a spray of white-heads blossoming under the skin across his nose and a tiny scar under his left eye. His breath smelled stale on my face and neck.

"Don't imagine for one minute that you'll be lining up in front of the Melling Road crossing," he threatened. He was talking about the start of the Grand National and the famous cinder track which the horses have to cross. "It's not going to happen." His nose was practically touching mine and his eyes were ice cold.

"You'll have to kill me first," I managed to croak, even though my shoulders were heaving with fear and sweat prickled the palms of my hands. I jerked my head back in defiance. "You'll never stop me riding."

"Justina, is that you?" Mandy's voice carried round the side of the box. My knees almost buckled with relief. Barnes hissed under his breath and marched off towards the stables.

"What did he want?" Mandy gaped after him, taking in my face and the hat silk lying in the mud.

"Nothing."

"Well I'm sure he wasn't inviting you to his mother's tea party—" She broke off when when she saw my face and heard my shallow breathing.

14

"It's just a touch of asthma. You know, a pollen thing, I'll be all right in a minute."

"Justina, you don't have asthma and the pollen count must be zero. It's early spring!"

"I'm fine, don't fuss. What's in the bag?" I nodded brusquely at a red plastic bag she was holding.

Mandy scowled, knowing I was deliberately changing the subject, but she couldn't resist filling me in on her latest pet project. "It's a 'Murphy' sweatshirt for Billy Piper."

"Billy Piper's asked for one?"

"Well, not exactly, but I've spotted her looka-like in the hospitality tent. Got to speculate to accumulate – I've even posted one to the Queen."

Somehow I couldn't see the Queen doing her next birthday tour with Murphy's image plastered on her front. Part of the proceeds from the fan club were going to the Injured Jockeys' Fund and the Racehorse Rehabilitation Centre.

With sickening dread I realized I could soon be a direct recipient. Was Dougie Barnes just using scare tactics or did he really mean to do harm?

Three

U

A misty, spring sun was a long way from rising when, a week later, Murphy clattered out of the yard for a piece of serious work up on the gallops. It was freezing cold, with just a few streaks of grey glinting through the heavy blackness. Other horses in the yard looked over their stable doors and whinnied, wondering what was gong on. We were extra early to avoid being spotted by journalists desperate to report back to readers the form of the big red horse. I doubted this would stop them. Badger, the head lad, had caught two in their car at the bottom of the drive, with a telescope trained on Murphy's stable. The whole racing world wanted to know if Murphy, and a sixteen-year-old female jockey, were capable of winning the Grand National.

Moments later the first horse broke the skyline, moving in a fluid, unrelenting gallop. The Guv'nor raised a pair of binoculars and traced its every stride. I shivered and felt a huge grin break on my face. The sound of galloping hooves always gave me a thrill but this morning the jockey crouched low on the withers of the horse was my boyfriend, Rory Calligan. I couldn't drink in enough of him – his tousled dark hair and good looks were like an oasis.

I hadn't seen him for weeks.

The Guv'nor was keen to get on with the job in hand. Always as nervous as a deer on the gallops in case anything happened to his precious charges, he habitually ran his hands down their slim, thoroughbred legs, feeling for any heat or swelling. Chelsea, his wire-haired terrier, would always be close by, more ferocious than any Rottweiler.

We were to canter for twenty minutes upsides, in other words, beside another horse, and then I was to take the lead and let Murphy run up the straight and tackle the hill. "Make sure he has a good blow, but don't overcook him. I want him out of breath but not exhausted." The air was laced with excitement. Most of the stable staff had come out and now stood along the track, keen to see the stable star in action. This was the moment of truth – to see whether the fall at the races had affected his action or confidence. I picked up the reins and rode alongside Rory's bay horse, not saying a word, breathless in the crisp air.

"Hello, gorgeous. Come here often?" Rory winked and slipped into a canter. Murphy half-reared, squealed, corkscrewed into a buck and went flying off in the lead.

I pulled him back in line with Rory, but only just. We shot past one of the furlong markers far too fast. Murphy was bursting with life. He wanted to eat up the ground. He was itching to leave his stable companion for dust and it took every iota of concentration to keep him hooked back. I thought of Grand National winners; of Red Rum beating Crisp; Red Rum winning for the third time; Aldaniti and jockey Bob Champion; Corbière, like Murphy, a chestnut. And I knew with heart-stopping gut instinct that we could make it work. I could be the youngest girl to win the biggest race of all time. Murphy was going to rewrite history.

All too soon we were pulling back, easing up from a burning gallop. The two horses snorted in unison. Rory's horse was sweating and done for and Murphy kept glancing across and tossing his head as if he was pleased with himself. Murphy's power could drain the confidence of any racehorse run against him. I patted his iron-hard neck appreciatively and grinned at Rory. "He's never felt better. I don't think he's ever worked so well."

The Guv'nor obviously thought so too because his usually-sceptical eyes gleamed with confidence.

The skill in training a top racehorse was, for

him, to see the horse peak on the day of his big race. Nobody was better than the Guv'nor at feeling for the right moment. Everyone at Dolphin Barn knew that morning that, bar a loose horse or a pile-up, Murphy would be at the Liverpool elbow with the Grand National finishing line in sight, before anything else on four legs.

Rory nodded encouragement. It had taken us a long time to achieve mutual respect for each other as jockeys and not fight over rides. I now knew without a shadow of a doubt that Rory would be cheering me on from the bottom of his heart. Murphy was my fate, my chance, but Rory's would come ten times over. He was a talented and accomplished jockey.

The smell of bacon and eggs wafted from the stable kitchen as we clattered into the yard. Murphy always insisted on being untacked outside and left loose to go into his stable, usually after visiting all the other horses and pinching carrots from Badger's feed trolley.

"I've missed you," Rory slung an arm round my shoulder. I buried my head into his sheepskin coat and cursed racing and the distance it put between us. Underneath the thick coat he was skin and bone. It was from constant dieting. Nobody worked harder than Rory – he wanted to be the next Richard Dunwoody and that meant total dedication.

"Hey, guys, put each other down quick and get in here – they're going over the runners for Aintree," shouted Larry, one of the stable lads, from the canteen where the television was blaring. Scooby was sliding bacon butties across the counter, but they were ignored as everyone congregated in front of the black-and-white screen.

"I don't believe it. That Russian horse is ten to one!" Larry sat on Jake's knee in his effort to get a better view. There was a hush as John Francome commented on the big black horse that had been sent over specially from Russia. "*This horse makes Desert Orchid look like a donkey. I've never seen a racehorse so tough and lean. He's the equine equivalent of James Bond. He'll eat Murphy's Law for breakfast.*"

There was a howl from the back and a slither of bacon slapped against the television screen, thrown by Scooby in an act of protest. Simultaneous grunts and groans highlighted the mutinous mood as the picture flashed to a Newmarket stables. Nobody, not even John Francome, was allowed to say anything against Murphy.

There was a sudden hush as the television showed the black Russian-bred racehorse set off up a strip of mown turf like a bullet. All our buoyant confidence and euphoria of moments earlier vanished. We sat in a trance and watched the black invader scorch up an incline, eating up some schooling fences as if they were beginners' jumps, *cavaletti*.

"*I've never seen anything like this horse in thirty years of training*," Nicky Henderson raved.

Nobody could pronounce its ridiculously long Russian name, so the horse was labelled The Black. "*The secret weapon to take on Murphy's Law*," John Oaksey burbled rapturously. Not so secret now, I thought, gloomily.

What would the Guv'nor think of it? Was he in his office now watching? This was what made the Grand National so special. It made fairy tales come true – Bob Champion fighting illness, Jenny Pitman, first woman trainer, Justina Brooks – youngest female jockey?

I felt nauseous as a fleeting image of losing crossed my mind. Winning the Grand National was what I'd lived and worked for since the age of thirteen when I'd skived off a part-time hairdressing job and jumped on a coach to Aintree. I still had the clod of turf I'd dug from the ground at Bechers Brook. Even now I could hear the thundering hooves, smell the excitement. And now I was going back – as a jockey and to win.

A wave of shock ran through me as the picture cut to a familiar face. It was Dougie Barnes. My mouth went dry. He was standing next to The Black and talking to the presenter but the sound had cut out and his mouth was just opening and

21

closing, making him look like a fish. The presenter nodded, mouthing another question. Larry thumbed frantically at the remote control, trying to get the sound operating.

Suddenly it blared out, full volume. *"You've won the Irish National three times. Is it going to be your year for the Grand National?"*

"I'm riding the best horse out of thirty-seven runners. I don't see why not. If I was one of the other jockeys, I'd be seriously worried."

It was as if he was sending me a message. A chorus of booing rose from the lads. Dougie Barnes was about as popular as a rattlesnake in a bath tub. But he was the one I had to beat.

With hare-like speed I shot out of the canteen and disappeared into the cottage which Mandy and I shared. In the mirror above the fridge I caught a glimpse of a face drained of colour. I was sweating and breathing in short gasps. The terror of my last encounter with Dougie Barnes kept flashing back, ever clearer and more frightening. I could remember each split second of panic. My neck was fine again now, but when I thought how easily I could have broken it . . .

"Justina Brooks get a grip!" I actually slapped my face, then glugged down a mug of cold water. I had to beat this.

The answerphone was flashing, telling me there was a message waiting. I pressed the button.

"Justina, it's your mother here. I'm not going to be put off any longer. I want to meet Rory in the flesh and see the cottage. It can't possibly be any worse than last time. I'll be there next Thursday with your brothers. Remember it's their birthday."

"That's all I need," I groaned. "My mother!" I couldn't cope with this. I was dying to see my twin brothers, I didn't mind introducing Rory, but the cottage? It looked as if it had been burgled twice then taken over by squatters. The only cleaning product it had ever seen was a bottle of horse shampoo that we'd used to get black tar off Smokey the cat. I think Mandy had finished it off as washing-up liquid.

This was drastic. It would take a team of industrial cleaners a whole month even to uncover the furniture. It would never be up to my mother's high standards of cleanliness by Thursday. She'd go ballistic.

Frantically, I started dusting the mantelpiece with my sleeve and scooping up a stack of free newspapers which had never been looked at, but had provided a wonderful coffee-table. I didn't dare look at the sink which was piled high with gloopy plates and mugs.

Rory slammed the back door and Poppy, his huge black-and-white Great Dane, galloped into the room and leaped straight on to the pile of newspapers, sending them skidding in all directions.

"What on earth are you doing?" Rory stared in alarm as I pulled the cushions off the settee, uncovering three mouldy socks and a dog's chewy bone. Poppy seemed ecstatic.

"My mother wants to meet you." I pulled two hair bands, a belt and a leadrope from down the back of the settee.

"What has that got to do with the settee?"

"Everything!" I screeched, knowing that, deep down, I was running away from the real issue. It was easier to think about cleaning the cottage than think about Dougie Barnes and the Grand National.

Rory raked back his hair, looking at me in confusion. He had the kind of smouldering, dark eyes that melted your heart. I knew lying to him would be the hardest thing I'd ever done.

"Justina, what's going on? The lads have just told me that Dougie Barnes deliberately ran you off the track yesterday. Is it true?"

"No! No definitely not. Nothing like that. It was me, I missed my line, I rode like a fool and expected too much of Murphy. I really blew it." I rolled my eyes for emphasis.

"So how come you're not watching the video over and over again and beating yourself up about it like you usually do? You're like a bear with a sore head when you've ridden badly."

I opened my mouth, hesitated, and then grasped at straws. "Maturity." I folded my arms. "No point getting steamed up. Can't change it." The silence dragged out. I twiddled my hair.

"Well thank heavens for that," Rory said after a minute. He seemed to buy the story. He stepped forward and encircled me in his arms, brushing his lips over my hair. "None of the older jockeys will talk about it, but Dougie Barnes is bad news. I'm not making this up, Jus, he's a real thug. Even I'd be scared to take him on."

A bucket-load of ice cubes cascaded into my stomach. "You've heard he's riding the favourite, the Russian horse called The Black?" My voice rose with nerves.

"He won't try anything in the race, not with half the world watching and cameras trained on you so close that they're practically picking out the hairs up your nose. You'll be as safe as houses. I can guarantee it."

I buried my face in Rory's shoulder and clung to his waist, as if we were about to bungee jump. He couldn't protect me for the time between now and the race, though. All the hours of build-up. How could I tell him now, after what he'd said, that I was frightened for my life?

Four

U

"That will be . . .". The shop assistant pointed at the till screen because I'd deliberately asked her not to say the amount out loud. I flattened my chequebook and proceeded to write a cheque for an amount which would mean no new jodhpurs or lipstick for a year.

"Are you sure this is what five-year-olds want?" I glanced dubiously at Tracy Island in a huge colourful box, and a bucket-load of balloons, puppets, masks and party poppers. Could children's presents really cost this much?

I caught the bus back to Dolphin Barn, thinking of my little brothers' faces. Maybe they'd like to see Murphy? Mum and Dad had fought me every step of the way to becoming a jockey. Both lawyers, they had expected that I'd go to university. It had horrified them when the racehorse "mania", as they called it, hadn't worn off. It was like an alien language to them. And when they'd seen where I was to live, and the work I would have to do for so little pay . . . But now they were proud of what I had achieved, and we seemed to be growing close again, like we were before.

As soon as I turned up the drive I could sense something different, a buzz of excitement. Then I saw the BBC cars and I knew what it was all about. They were showing a preview on the Wednesday night before the Grand National and had been filming all of the main contenders. Now it was Murphy's turn. They'd want to see him galloping and me all fresh-faced and exhilarated. Adrenaline coursed into my bloodstream – this is what I'd dreamed about since my first ride on a horse.

The Guv'nor was striding up and down the yard with his hair stuck out like electrified steel wool. Chelsea was barking from an empty stable to which he'd obviously been banished. A blonde television girl was leaning especially close to Rory, flirting with him so obviously that it was a wonder he didn't faint.

"She's here." Badger, the head lad, spotted me first and then dived out of the way. The Guv'nor approached something close to a smile and didn't even comment on my shopping bags.

"They had to change the time," he said, barely moving his smiling lips. "Now get your engine into gear before they change their minds as well."

It was the first time I'd taken a few hours off for

over two and a half months. I couldn't believe that something like this could happen. In a frenzy I dived into the tackroom and pulled on jodhpurs and chaps and tucked my green tinted hair into a jockey skullcap, which is racing's equivalent to a riding hat. I had to look professional. Thousands of people would be tuning in to decide which horse to back. I had to look better than Dougie Barnes and The Black.

"What will you do if you fall at the first fence?" They were recording an interview with me before they filmed us on the gallops.

"Try again next year?"

"What makes you think you can do better than Gee Armitage and any other girl jockey?"

"I've got a special horse."

"Are you frightened of Bechers Brook and Valentines fences?"

"More scared of the Chair. It's the tallest and narrowest fence on the course."

"Are you fit enough to stand up to the four-mile, four-furlong course?"

"I can swim one hundred and fifty laps and do three hundred sit-ups before breakfast."

"Do you think you're good enough to take on Dougie Barnes and The Black?"

Words dried up in my throat. I stared at the camera for awkward moments and then, thankfully, Murphy butted me in the back, which relieved the tension. "I think he's saying yes, we are," I laughed, rubbing at his sheepskin noseband.

"Red Rum is your favourite horse of all time. Are you trying to make Murphy his double by riding him in a sheepskin noseband?"

"No not really. It's there for a purpose, to encourage him to lower his head and look at his fences. He tends to be too reckless otherwise."

"Who are backing for the race?"

"That would be telling." I winked at the camera and someone shouted, "Cut", and it was all over. Murphy immediately went back to his haynet, as if he knew he was no longer centre stage. I was glad one of us was calm because my knees were shaking.

"That was great. I hope you win." Andy, who sported three earrings through one eyebrow and had done the filming, shook my hand. I just hoped he didn't notice how sweaty it was.

"What is the security like here?" Mark, who was in charge of sound, glanced around, presumably looking for security cameras.

"Um, well, there's a central alarm system and floodlights, and then there's Gertie, nobody would get past her in a hurry." I pointed to the obstinate goat that Larry was leading round the yard in an effort to keep her from sabotaging the film or, at the very least, butting the camera crew.

"She would die for Murphy rather than let anything happen to him."

"She might have to, I mean, if anyone were to break in. You hear all sorts of stories, about fancied horses being got at and stuff. I'm amazed you don't have a camera in his stable."

I shuffled uncomfortably. I didn't want even to contemplate the thought . . .

"Have you seen The Black?" I blurted out, unable to help myself.

Mark's eyes lit up. "He's awesome." There was a tone of reverence in his voice that made my heart sink. "His jockey's a bit of an idiot, though. Kept going on about how he was going to win, whatever it took."

A cold shudder ran down my spine. "I expect he thinks he can," I mumbled, and turned back to unclip Murphy's headcollar, wishing I hadn't brought the subject up.

"You've got to tell him!" Mandy dogged me like Poppy, only she was worse because I couldn't throw her a stick to get rid of her.

"I will not!" I repeated for the fiftieth time.

"You're my best friend and you're walking around looking terrified. How many times have you glanced out of the window tonight? You jump at the slightest noise, never mind if someone knocks at the door. "You're a nervous wreck."

To prove her point Mandy stood on top of the toilet and opened the window, releasing a tiny piece of silver foil that I'd stuck there so I'd know if anyone broke into the cottage.

"OK, so you've made your point, but I'm still not telling him. I don't want it getting out that as soon as I have a problem I run to my boyfriend for help. I'll be a laughing stock in the weighing room. They'll never take me seriously. I've got to stand on my own two feet."

"Until you get knocked off them by somebody twice your size. Didn't you learn anything when Murphy was being threatened before? It was only sorted out once you told people what was going on." She disappeared into her room.

"What did you say about being knocked off my feet?" I called from my room.

"Nothing, nothing. What looks best? Black or red, and be honest." Mandy appeared at my door. She held up two dresses. It was Ben's birthday and we were meeting at the Jockey's Rest, a pub in the village, for a special curry night. About half a dozen other jockeys would be there, all intent on giving Ben the bumps or at least swapping his mild Korma curry for a very hot vindaloo. The racing fraternity was addicted to practical jokes and I knew we wouldn't get through the night without some high pranks.

"The red," I said. I pulled on some old black

31

trousers so as not to upstage Mandy. "If you really want to help me," I grimaced, coming out of my room, "you can find somebody to clean this place up." I gestured at the mess and clutter which seemed to spread like spilled wine. "If my mother sees this . . ." With six o'clock starts, non-stop work and cold weather, neither of us was in any mood for picking up a brillo pad.

"Oh, that's all sorted," Mandy waved away my concern. "We've got our very own cleaner starting tomorrow morning." She reached for the green nail varnish, looking very smug.

"Who?" I demanded, imaging a stooped old lady from the village, with a hair-net and false teeth. "I hope it's nobody who's going to snoop through my things."

"Oh, yes," Mandy flicked green specks on the duvet without realizing it. "He'll have a ball. You'd better hide any love letters pronto and any frilly knickers, unless you want them paraded in the weighing room."

"He? Who, Mandy?"

"Calm down, don't turn your hair any greener. It's Davido. He came round to use the washing machine and volunteered for the job. Said he's been dying to plunge our sink for weeks and how could we live in such filth and dilapidation."

"Davido? Is he mad?"

"No madder than any other jockey I've met. What does my hair look like?"

"You look gorgeous. Where's my purse?" We filed out of the back door, me taking extra care to lock it properly and arrange the mat so I'd know if it had been moved. Mandy was too busy looking in her compact to notice.

"Oh, talking about your purse," she moved a few steps away. "I don't think I mentioned, Davido wants ten pounds an hour and I agreed."

"What?" I charged forward at full tilt, ready to strangle her, and instead broke a heel and nearly strangled myself on the washing-line.

Practically everybody at Dolphin Barn stampeded out of the back of the horsebox when it pulled up outside the Jockey's Rest. Mandy and I had at least been allowed to travel in the relative comfort of the cab next to Scooby. I felt sorry for Mandy, who had desperately wanted a romantic evening for two and instead was having to put up with half the Cheltenham racing fraternity. She closed her eyes in horror as Ben crashed through the pub door with Sharpie O'Hare and Daryl Hamley. He was wearing a pair of Union Jack boxer shorts over his trousers and a children's riding hat back to front. He had a false ginger moustache on his face and a leadrope round his neck. Everybody whooped and made a dive to give him the bumps.

Mandy's face crumpled as Ben's arms and legs went in all directions and he disappeared behind a barstool.

My heart soared when the front door swung open and Rory walked in, causing every girl in the pub to glance in his direction. Up till then I'd been watching the door like it was a hen about to lay a golden egg, hoping he'd make it back from Cardiff races. He looked tired and pale and in need of a shave.

"Hey, is that your boyfriend?" A girl in a low top at the next table whispered across as if a film star had just walked in. Even if I said yes, I got the feeling she was about to leap into his arms and cover him in crimson lipstick. Rory, totally oblivious, came over and gave me a kiss before going to order drinks at the bar.

When he came and sat down, he gave me a look which privately asked how long we needed to stay before we could leave without looking rude. Mandy had her head down, shredding a beer mat with one hand and dabbing her waterproof mascara with the other. Ben hadn't surfaced yet from the bumps, which seemed to be stretching into eternity.

"How did you get on today?" I asked Rory.

"Two wins and a third." He rubbed a hand across his forehead and down the side of his temple. "Had to practically carry them though."

I'd seen one race on television and Rory had made an average horse look superb. It would probably never win a race again, not with a less superior jockey. Rory tipped back his mineral water. I knew all he would have eaten today was ice cubes and sugarfree chewing-gum. He lived on scraps to make the weights.

"He'll never stay!" A group of our stable lads were arguing an each-way bet on the National.

"Oh come on, he ran well in the Hennessy Cup and that's over three miles two furlongs."

"Bull. That's like comparing an egg-and-spoon race with the London Marathon."

"There's only one horse going to win the National and that's Murphy's Law," Larry shouted in a Guinness-rich voice. A hush fell over the usually noisy room. Tension seemed to increase by the second. I bit my lip and closed my eyes. All over the country, in every pub, sitting-room, betting shop, post office, and corner shop, people were discussing our chances. It felt like the rock of Gibraltar swinging round my neck. The pressure was squeezing into my temples and twisting my stomach into knots. I just wanted to go home, forget all the speculation and be normal.

Rory's mobile phone bleeped just as everybody started talking again.

"I'm sorry, I've gotta go." He scooped up his car keys and scraped his chair back.

"Where? This minute?" A drizzle of panic crept into my voice.

"It's a trainer in Lambourn. Wants me to ride a horse on the Monday at Aintree."

"So?"

"He wants me to look at it now."

"But, Rory, it's dark. You're in Cheltenham, not Lambourn."

"Well, he's got an indoor school and I've got a fast car." The buzz of a new ride, another chance at a winner, took over. It was an addiction.

"How shall I get home?" I knew my voice sounded plaintive but I couldn't help it. There was no way I was climbing back in the horsebox with a load of drunken lads standing on my toes and breathing lager fumes.

"I'll take you home." Davido, who had sat down at our table when he came in a few moments earlier, took his car keys out of his pocket.

"Oh spare me the highway robbery man."

"I've got a Porsche and a good heater and fur seat covers and I haven't had anything to drink."

"You'll be fine with Davido," Rory pecked me on the cheek and grabbed his coat.

I knew I would be fine with Davido, but that wasn't the point. I wanted to be with Rory. I'd have to metamorphose into a racehorse to spend more than a fleeting hour with him. Tears stung the back of my eyes. I gritted my teeth.

"You not happy with me cleaning your house?" Davido eyed me questioningly. "I bring my own vacuum and duster." His Italian accent and the mention of a Porsche caught the ear of the girl in the low top.

"You can come and clean for me, love, anytime." She winked at me and pushed past, tousling Davido's black hair."

"I'd like to go sooner rather than later," I feigned a yawn. "Like now. Immediately. This minute." I looked around for Mandy but she was over by the bar being talked into a game of darts by Larry. Her shoulders sagged and she looked as disappointed romantically as I felt.

Davido drove like Rory, which was like a Grand Prix driver. The car squealed round wet corners as he roared through the gears. Jockeys, according to sports psychologists, are addicted to speed but I'd have been quite happy in a Reliant Robin. Davido was telling me about home delicacies back in Italy. "Here, you have pork scratchings, back home we have boiled nerves in big pot on the stove, mmm!" He kissed his fingers. I felt my stomach lurch.

It seemed light years before we pulled up at Dolphin Barn. Davido suddenly flung his head on to the steering wheel in a dramatic pose. I jumped sharply.

"I have something to get off my chest. I need to tell you. That's why I volunteer to clean your house, so I can see you."

For a horrifying moment I thought he was going to declare undying love. Within seconds I was mentally rehearsing what I was going to say, so as not to break his passionate Italian heart.

He lifted his head and stared at the batting windscreen wipers. "I feel like a bad man for not telling you this sooner, but they all make pact, say nothing, it's all in the past."

I cleared my throat nervously. "Davido, don't keep me in suspense. What are you trying to say?"

"I'm saying that Dougie Barnes is a dangerous man. Eight years ago he put beautiful young girl in wheelchair and showed no remorse. He rode into her like he did you and she break back. There was big cover-up. He retired, and then last year, he start race riding again. But he's same man underneath. He's mean, he'll do anything to win and he hates girl jockeys. Please, Justina, don't ride in the National, you're in real danger. He's a psych . . . psycho – what you say?"

"Davido, who knows about this?" My voice, amazingly, had gone up only a couple of notes. I was surprised I was able to speak.

"The other jockeys. Sharpie O'Hare remembers

the race and the girl. Ben Le Sueur's father rode in the race. But Rory doesn't know. They think if they say nothing it will go away, that Barnes can't be that stupid again. They all frightened of him."

"Thanks for telling me." Mechanically, I unclicked the seat belt and levered myself out of the car.

"You going to ride?" An edge of panic grated in his voice.

"What do you think?" I answered.

The Porsche swerved away through a puddle as I walked up to the cottage and disappeared into the darkness. I let myself in and stood against the back door, heaving with fear. Every nerve strained to hear anything out of the ordinary. But there was nothing. Just Smokey, keen to miaow hello and weave around my legs. I let out a long breath and leaned down to stroke him. "If there's such a thing as telepathy," I whispered hoarsely, "Rory Calligan will be flying back up the motorway to Dolphin Barn now."

But I knew that was unlikely. He was chasing a winner and a dream. I was on my own and terrified beyond reason.

Five

♘

"I want you to practise the Canal Turn," the Guv'nor ran his hands over Murphy, instinctively feeling for any tension, any taut muscles, the slightest heat spot.

Outside, the rain poured down in blinding sheets. It was National week and if this kept up, the going would be heavy to mudlike. Murphy was a huge horse and the heavy ground would sap his strength. We couldn't race four and half miles in sinking conditions.

The Guv'nor and I both knew it. He was wound up like a spring. Lines of tension had suddenly appeared on his face, like cracks in dry ground. The pressure was enormous. Only that morning the racing papers had been full of speculation – a horse-by-horse guide to the world's greatest steeplechase. It seemed that everywhere I looked, I'd see Justina Brooks and the famous black-and-burgundy colours of Dolphin Barn.

Roy, one of the stable lads, passed a quarter

sheet over the stable door, causing Murphy to jerk backwards.

"You stupid, dense idiot!" The Guv'nor flew at him. "Haven't you heard of strained muscles? And this isn't even the right sheet. I said the waterproof one, you oafhead. How many times do I have to tell you?" The Guv'nor shoved the quarter sheet back in Roy's chest, then grabbed it back and stamped it into the wet sludgy concrete. "Now clean that up and stack it back neatly."

A ripple of horror passed through everybody in the yard. The Guv'nor was a brilliant, passionate trainer but he could be a bad-tempered bully with a fanatical obsession for his horses. I felt so sorry for Roy, who blushed scarlet and stumbled away, probably feeling as if he'd been bitten by a cobra.

"That wasn't fair," I said and immediately regretted it as the Guv'nor lasered me with narrowed, piercing eyes.

"If you've got something to prove as a jockey," the Guv'nor raised his chin, "I suggest you fasten your hat and get out there and prove to the world that you can handle the toughest test in racing."

"Why didn't he tell me?" I fumed to Scooby, who was riding upsides on Tralligan.

Mark and Andy had come back for some extra film footage and were parked halfway up the gallops, where the lads had simulated a Grand

National fence by laying straw on top of an ordinary fence to build up the height. The thought of being filmed at this time of the morning *and* being expected to jump as well was too much. I hadn't had a chance to psych myself up.

Mark and Andy were dressed as if they were going white-water rafting and even the camera had its own raincoat. To add insult to injury, they insisted I took off my coat and rode in Dolphin Barn colours. My teeth chattered and my fingers felt frozen round the reins. Murphy arched his back and bucked furiously as the rain trickled down his mane and neck in rivulets. My back ached and my brain felt numb. I hadn't slept a wink last night after what Davido had told me. His words kept spinning round my head in a relentless cycle.

The Guv'nor's orders were clear in my mind. After I'd warmed up in a half-gallop alongside Tralligan I was to turn back and negotiate the jump, with a sharp left-hand turn on landing, just like the Canal Turn at Aintree. Steering was never one of our hot spots and Murphy was naturally unbalanced on the left.

"Grip with your lower knees. Keep your head and shoulders low. Don't pull on the horse's mouth. Don't keep your reins too tight . . ." The Guv'nor barked out instructions. Chelsea, keen to be part of the action, suddenly ran out in front of the fence, legs going like the clappers and yapping hysterically.

"Cut!" Andy frantically polished the lens of the camera. I hadn't even started my run up.

"Get that blasted dog back in the car," the Guv'nor shouted, but he was forced to do it himself after Scooby said, with some defiance, that he'd rather pick up a piranha.

Murphy and I started our run up. I never failed to be in awe of his massive strength. He powered through the deep ground and leaped over a smaller fence as if he were jumping from a spring-board. A swell of excitement filled my chest.

We steered round for the Canal Turn jump. Murphy's ears pricked.

"OK, boy, all we've got to do is jump and turn ninety degrees in the air. It's a piece of cake." We set off at a blistering gallop, as straight as an arrow. Usually in eventing or showjumping there is enough time to set the horse up. But not in the Grand National. Thirty or more horses would surge into the fence without a pause. There would be knocks and pile-ups and falls. It was all about survival and quick wits. It was more than just riding. It was a union between horse and rider.

Every pair of eyes was trained on the fence. There was no noise, not a breath. Murphy set himself like a spring ready to uncoil. Every sinew tensed, every muscle in his quarters bulged, ready to thrust him forward.

We were nearly there. Three, two, one. He stretched upwards. He didn't notice the rain, he was doing what he did best – jumping into orbit with a power and scope hardly seen before. He was an Arkle, a Red Rum, a champion, and he responded to me. I'd nurtured his talent.

"What was that?" The Guv'nor growled under his breath, shaking slightly so his mouth twitched, as we rode back to him.

We had missed the turn altogether. Murphy hadn't understood what I'd asked and we'd over-shot by lengths. I couldn't believe how difficult it was. A new uncertainty diluted my confidence.

"Do you know what that would mean in the race?" The Guv'nor put a leathery hand on Murphy's bridle, holding him still. "You'll be left for dead. You'll be out of the race and miles behind. End of story. Blown. Lost. Wasted. You've got to be sharp. You've got to be hugging that inside rail and opening your left rein as soon as you feel his shoulders come off the ground. It happens in seconds. You get two chances – it's fence eight on the first circuit and the twenty-fourth on the second. On a tired horse in heavy going you'll practically have to carry him over. He relies on you to be a good jockey. You can't sit there filing your nails."

We tried again and again. Each time we were tighter, more together, twisting in the air. Murphy got the idea. I was concentrating so hard I didn't notice the camera still rolling. Everyone was locked into sharing something special, training a great horse, an intense moment and a glimpse of what was to come.

The Guv'nor knew every trick. Each suggestion, order, adjustment was fine tuning us for perfection. The Guv'nor knew every blade of grass on the Aintree course.

"I left this until now," he explained, "to shock you into action. I want the Canal Turn to be fresh in your mind on Saturday. You'll not mess up in a hurry now."

Not for the first time I thought what a brilliant trainer he was. He instinctively knew how to get the best out of jockeys and horses. And this was his personal crusade too. It was over twenty years since he'd trained a National winner. Other, younger trainers thought he was past it, over the hill. He had something to prove as much as I did.

"That was amazing." Andy had carefully put the camera back in the car and he and Mark picked their way across to the massive fence. Clouds of steam were rising off Murphy but he wasn't a bit out of breath. He circled wildly, just wanting to get back to the job. His nostrils flared the colour of poppies and the rain mingled with sweat to turn his coat almost black.

Nobody seemed to notice the cold and the wet.

"That was brilliant! Just what the viewers want!" Both men were bowled over with the film. "It's going out on Wednesday night, straight after the usual run down of the favourites. We'll call it Race to Glory."

"Isn't that assuming too much? Assuming that we'll win?"

There was no mention of The Black now. The Russian contender had dropped into insignificance. I noticed the Guv'nor eyeing Mark's green jumper which came into view as his coat blew open. The Guv'nor was fiercely superstitious and wouldn't let anyone at Dolphin Barn wear green, believing it to be bad luck. He wouldn't relish the coincidence just as we were discussing Murphy's chances. We all knew that to win the National you needed skill and dedication and valour. But you also needed luck on your side. Pots of it.

For the first time it crossed my mind how tired the Guv'nor looked. Preparation for the race was taking its toll. Despite everyone being on a high he walked back to his four-wheel drive with a tense face and the stooped shoulders of an old man.

*

"Can I buy you a drink?" I'd sneaked off to the Jockey's Rest at lunchtime with the sole intention of bumping into Sharpie O'Hare. He was standing at the end of the bar, rolling a cigarette carefully between forefinger and thumb. I scrunched up my eyes against the smoky, dim light and reached into my pocket.

"A pint of Guinness would hit the spot, all right."

Sharpie O'Hare was one of the oldest jockeys still riding. He'd been brought up in Belfast and learned to ride with no saddle and just a rope for a bridle on the ponies kept on common land. Like all of us, he'd started off working in a stables, trying to get his talent noticed. For every stable lad who became a jockey there were thousands who didn't. Last year he'd had a terrible accident at a water jump and nearly died. Since then he had been struggling to get rides and everyone in the business was trying to persuade him to pack it in. I passed the money for a pint of Guinness over the counter and asked if we could sit at a table.

"So, what you have come to ask me, then? To see my special party trick or to find out how to ride Bechers?"

I grimaced at the first suggestion. Sharpie had dislocated his collar bone so many times that he could slip it out of its socket and swivel it round so it looked as if his arm was attached back to front.

"Bechers then?" He ran on. "Let me see. Fourteen Nationals and never fallen at the Brook, that must be some kind of record."

Even though that wasn't what I'd really come for, I couldn't help but soak up his information like a sponge. Sharpie had been a top jockey with so much experience that that's how he'd acquired his nickname.

"Bechers is different from any other fence at Aintree, and not just because of the drop – and believe me, that can put you in a neck brace for weeks. No, it's on a bend, see? And as you come in, it feels like you're gonna jump into the crowd on the right hand side. There's lots of noise, shouting, screaming and it takes a horse's mind off the job, especially if he's a front runner like your chap. He'll be too busy listening to the crowd to notice the drop. I'd say Bechers is your bogey fence, all right. Get the lad over that and you might do a clear circuit."

"But no more?" I gave him a glare.

He shrugged. "Just the mere mention of the letters G and N sees most jump jockeys knotting up with tension. I've seen grown men reduced to tears after walking that course. It's rough, tough, hellish. Why do you want to do it? It's not Pony Club land, you know."

I bristled internally but forced my mouth to smile. All the while I was more determined than ever. "Maybe you're more worried about who wants to hurt me?" I let my voice fall away.

He stiffened immediately.

"You've been mates with Dougie Barnes for years. You must know everything that's gone on."

"Not mates, associates. And I haven't talked to him properly for weeks."

"But you must know about the accident, what the girl's name was?"

Only a small twitch at the side of his mouth betrayed his nervousness, but his eyes gave me the feeling that he was scrambling around for something to say. "I don't know nothing. I had a fall, remember? There's some things I can't recall."

"That's funny, you did all right recalling Bechers."

"Look, I don't know, OK." He half rose from his chair, slopping beer. I noticed that the knuckles of his hand gripping the glass were white. "You'll get nothing out of nobody. What's past is past. To be left alone." He drained his glass and stood up. "Can I get you a drink before I go?"

Disappointment and confusion at his reaction slowed my responses. What was going on? "Uh, no," I eventually answered. "I don't drink. I'm under age."

*

49

"Where's the Yellow Pages?" I turned all the cushions on the settee upside down and then started on the magazine rack which was overflowing with form books and old copies of *Horse and Hound* magazine.

Mandy was sprawled on the floor, using a pair of trimming scissors meant for fetlocks to cut out a pattern for a Hawaiian shirt for Ben. Smokey was just about to knock over a tin of pins and give himself home acupuncture. She'd have to do more than make Ben a shirt to get to Mauritius. Ben was known for having barbed wire round his wallet. And round his heart I thought, considering he hadn't breathed a word about Barnes and obviously didn't intend to. I scooped up Smokey in the nick of time and resorted to Directory Enquiries.

"Blast!"

"What?"

"Um, nothing." I chewed frantically at my thumbnail. I'd just tried ringing Cheltenham library to see if I could scan old newspapers, but they were closed for a week for refurbishment. The local paper had a research department, but it would take a few days to trace the relevant papers and they were short-staffed.

I didn't dare tell Mandy what Davido had said. She'd go straight to Rory and the Guv'nor and it might cause a row between her and Ben if she found out that he'd kept quiet. Although the Guv'nor probably knew about the accident, he had no idea that Dougie Barnes was threatening me.

There was something in my bones that told me that Barnes really meant it. He could just be trying psychological tactics in the hope that I'd crumble on the day, but I was his main rival. We both had a die-hard desperation to win the National. I'd already had a taste of the lengths he'd go to, and Davido wasn't worried for nothing. He genuinely thought I was putting myself at risk.

I felt like I was clutching at straws but if I could just find out about the injured girl, the race, why the other jockeys were covering up . . .

"I was trying to find out something about the National," I half-lied to Mandy. "From the reference library." If she smelled a rat, she'd never leave it alone. Luckily, she was more interested in matching up garish buttons from a biscuit tin full of them that her gran had sent her.

"Why go to the library when we've got our very own Mastermind in the yard?"

"Sorry?"

"Badger," she grinned. "I think he was around when they first created the thoroughbred. He certainly never gets anything wrong in the pub quiz anyway."

51

"Mandy, you beauty!" I kissed the top of her head. "What a brilliant idea."

"Oh, and I asked Ben about that Barnes bully. I said how frightened you were and he said there's no need to be. He's all hot air but some of the older lads have had a word with him and he'll not pull any more stunts. He wouldn't dare."

"Right." I wondered why I didn't feel at all reassured.

As head lad of the stables, in charge of all the staff and ninety racehorses, Badger had his own cottage on the estate. Not that he was ever there much. His life was the racing stables and the horses and nobody started work earlier or left later, whatever day of the week.

I knocked nervously on the porch door knowing that in an hour or so he'd be going back out to check all the horses last thing before bed. An owl hooted in a nearby tree and I could almost feel its beady eyes watching me. I shivered and pulled my coat closer. A light went on.

Badger shuffled the door open with some difficulty. It obviously didn't get much use. His eyes gave away his first thought, that something was wrong with one of the horses.

"It's all right. There is nothing wrong. I wanted to talk to you, that's all, if you don't mind. It won't take a minute."

Reluctantly, he opened the door wider and

ushered me in. I stepped straight into a tiny sitting room where the television was switched on and a sheet of newspaper lay by the settee. I had to wipe my feet on it. Even though the room was dimly lit, it was easy to see that it hadn't been changed for decades. I bet the kitchen still had a stone sink.

"So, I think I can guess what this is about."

"Yeah?" I caught my heel in a ruck in the carpet and stumbled, feeling really awkward.

"You'll be wanting to know about Dougie Barnes."

I couldn't believe that he knew what I had come for. He even volunteered the information easily, though with resignation. It was almost as if he enjoyed unlocking old memories. I couldn't get enough of what he had to say.

"It happened over eight years ago. The six-teenth of September. I remember the ground was rock-hard. She was a pretty lass but tougher than she was given credit for. She was a good rider, that's what really got up Dougie's nose. He'd been having a bad run and she beat him once in a bumper race. That was the turning point. He threatened to ride her off and nobody believed he'd do it. He waited until they were out in the woods and then he deliberately rode into her, causing her horse to somersault. She went down hard underneath. The horse was killed outright and she smashed her vertebrae. She ended up in a wheelchair. That was the end of Melody Phipps's racing career." Badger sucked in his cheeks and shook his head as if he was talking about a horse or a dog.

"But she is still alive?" I pressed.

"Oh, yeah. I wrote to her once. She and her mother moved up to Blackburn in Lancashire after it happened. I think they run a livery stable. Nice girl."

"But she never complained, I mean reported it?"

"Oh yeah, she wanted Dougie to be sent down, but the other jockeys closed ranks. They wouldn't testify. Said they hadn't seen anything during the race. Of course nobody was surprised, they weren't entirely without blame."

"What do you mean?"

"Dougie had whipped up Sharpie O'Hare and Kevin Le Sueur. They were his sidekicks. A few weeks before, they'd gone to her house in hats and masks, with flaming torches to frighten her. It went further than it was supposed to and that's when the lads realized what Dougie was at, but they were involved by then.

"Kevin was Ben Le Sueur's dad?"

"Yes, that's right. I think Ben has an inkling of what went on, but tries to hide the family skeletons."

I sat down as if my knees had buckled.

"I wouldn't worry." Badger's eyes narrowed slightly, almost with a hint of contempt. "He wouldn't try anything now, not after Sharpie's had a word, and certainly not with half the world tuning in to watch.

My stomach heaved. It was literally one of the biggest sporting events in the globe. The winner always enjoyed overnight fame. "But there's more ways than one to skin a cat," I croaked, trying to crease my lips into a smile.

Badger ignored me and stared instead at the oil painting above the fireplace. It was a replica of the one in the Guv'nor's office – of Dolphin, the horse the Guv'nor had trained to win the National.

"You don't want me to ride, do you?" I hadn't meant to say it, but now I was compelled to go on. "You don't believe I can do it either, you think a man should be riding him. It's written all over your face."

He didn't deny it. "I believe," he said, rubbing a hand over his whiskery chin, "that the Guv is a brilliant trainer of racehorses. He could train a goat to win a race and now he's got a second throw of the dice with a horse like Murphy. I just want him to have the best chance."

I didn't speak for a minute or two, just felt the rush of blood in my ears and throat. "Well, maybe I ought to remind you," I eventually managed to say in a hollow voice, "that Murphy wouldn't race with a man on his back, and if it wasn't for me sticking my neck out and risking my job, he wouldn't even be at Dolphin Barn. What was it you called him when we first saw him? 'A boat with four legs, a horse who couldn't win a race if it had a twenty-furlong head start?' Well, I think I've earned the right to be riding him on Saturday and I think you know it too. All that remains is for us to win – and we will!"

Outside, the freezing, black air doused my temper. I breathed in deeply and walked down the path, back to the beacon of light which was our kitchen window. I was calm but the heat of my belief was suddenly edged with lingering doubt. I had to face the thought. Could I really do justice to such a great horse, or was I biting off more than I could chew?

Six

U

"Are you all right?" It was Rory's husky voice. I'd picked up the phone on the third ring and now I was holding it to me like something precious.

"Where are you?"

"Bristol. I'm sitting outside a trainer's yard waiting for the first lot. They've got a horse running in the National and at the moment no jockey. It's a no-hoper, but at least I'd get the chance to go down the parade with you."

I couldn't speak. The thought of Rory riding with me in the great race was too much. The relief was enough to drown in.

"I had a dream last night that I fell at the first fence and all the crowds came on the racecourse and lynched me."

"Pre-great-race nerves," Rory answered. He was eating something. I could hear him peeling off the wrapper. I knew that I'd play this phone call back in my head for the rest of the day. Rory did something to me that nobody else could do. I felt warm and tingly.

"I've got a runner at Taunton, then I'll be back with you tonight. And from then on I'm all yours. Think of me as your own sports psychologist. I'll talk you through every fence. We'll watch videos with the Guv'nor. I'll have you so positive you won't be able to wait for that tape to fly up."

"Rory . . ." I could feel my eyes welling up.

"Sorry, babe. Gotta go. I can see the horses pulling out. See you tonight." The line went dead.

I closed my eyes.

I hadn't told him anything of Melody Phipps and what she'd endured. I hadn't told him that I'd been awake all night, tossing and turning and that self-doubt was creeping through me like a virus, blotting out all the good aspects of my riding. I hadn't told him that I didn't think I could go through with it . . .

The Guv'nor called me into his office at eight-thirty. Form books littered the desk and a congealed egg sandwich was waiting for me on the coffee table. "Eat," he ordered. "Brian Johnson's chipped his collar bone and can't ride for Eddy Newton at Nottingham in the seller." A seller was a race at which the horses were sold to the highest bidder after they had run.

I waited, wondering where this was leading. As I sank my teeth into the hard yolk I tried to ignore Chelsea, who slavered at my feet, making threatening noises.

"I said you could stand in."

"What?" Panic tore through my chest. "I won't," I retaliated flatly.

"Yes, you will. It's just what you need to take your mind off things. And it will sharpen you up for Saturday."

"What, journalists thrusting mikes at me and calling me National Velvet is just what I need?"

"You're a professional jockey, Justina, and that's part of the game. If it makes you feel any better," he added starchily, "Dougie Barnes is nowhere near the area."

This was my perfect chance to bring up Melody Phipps, to voice my rising fear but, instead, seconds slipped away and I just fiddled with some gritty shell in my bread roll. "Any riding instructions?" I asked, as I walked resignedly towards the door.

"Just one. Don't fall off."

The race was at Southwell on an all-weather track. The trainer, Eddie Newton, had organized a driver and car for me. If I hadn't been so stressed, I'd have enjoyed the VIP treatment.

"So, shall I put some money on your horse, then?" The driver gave me a grin as I picked up my racing saddle from the back seat. We'd swung into the main entrance and I was keeping an eye out for signs for the weighing room.

"Your guess is as good as mine," I grinned back, knowing he'd be disappointed at the lack of a good tip. "I haven't even seen the horse yet."

"Yeah, but they say all the nags fall in love with you, and all the fellas for that matter. I think I'll put my money on you all the same."

It was a gloomy afternoon, with darkness already round the corner. I found the travelling head lad in charge of Doogle Don, my ride for the race, and collected my riding colours, which were orange with a black hoop. Doogle Don was a chestnut gelding who looked cheesed off with life but perked up when I rubbed his ears and blew into his nose. I always do that when I meet a new horse. It creates a bond.

"He usually bites everyone who goes near him." The lad looked flummoxed and scratched his tousled hair. Something in me stirred then. I had a gift – I could feel it in my fingertips. An uncanny ability to get into a horse's head and ease his troubles, get him to do his best for me. Other people had noticed it, the Guv'nor for one, which is why he gave me a job when I was so young.

I'd earned my place here on the racecourse, through talent and dogged determination. The self-doubt and negative thoughts dropped away like a cloak. I wasn't going to let Dougie Barnes rob me of my race to glory. Saturday was my big day. Murphy's occasion. The whole country was locked into speculation about the huge red horse that nobody had wanted and the female jockey who had spotted his talent and risked her livelihood to acquire him. I quivered with nervous energy. It was as if a quick shot of adrenaline had suddenly jerked me awake. We could do it. We could win on Saturday, despite everything.

I headed for the weighing room with every nerve end zinging. I couldn't wait to get out on the racetrack, to feel the heady thrill that comes with burning up the home straight.

"Sorry, luv, your changing rooms are over there, just been refurbished. There's a special power shower for the lassies." The steward redirecting my path winked and grinned broadly. "In fact, you'll have it all to yourself today. There are no other lassies racing."

"Showers for the lassies? That's a shame," I shot back. "I rather like the communal ones."

He stared, uncertain whether I was joking and I imagined the sports headlines the next morning. *"Justina Joshes with Jockeys in Communal Shower."* The Guv'nor would go ape, not to mention Rory. I glanced at my watch. Jockeys had to be ready and on the scales at least fifteen minutes before the race started, otherwise the officials would issue a hefty fine. I had enough time. I decided to wear goggles to keep the mud from flicking into my eyes. A heavy drop of rain slid down my neck as I reached for the changing room door.

I didn't remember much else. I was shoved from behind and fell forward through the partly opened door. Despite knowing how to roll into a tight ball to protect myself, my head hit against a wooden trunk and stars flashed seconds before I blacked out. The only thing I was sure of was that I recognized the voice – at once and with stomach-wrenching fear. Dougie Barnes.

I came round moments later to feel his steel-like forearm locked against my windpipe. "Move!"

I was forced across the room and pressed into a chair. I could feel blood running into my hair. My brain was zigzagging with inane thoughts, unable to trigger the correct response to the situation. I giggled helplessly, knowing I was on a knife-edge and could cry as easily any minute.

Hearing me laugh incensed Dougie Barnes. With new roughness he jammed both my arms behind the back of the chair and started binding my wrists together so that the heels of my hands burned with pain and the cord he used sliced mercilessly into the soft flesh of the inside of my wrists.

"The more you fight it the worse it will pull." He tied a knot on top of two others and then

stepped round to face me. There were tiny drop-
lets of perspiration on his forehead and veins
bulging in his thick neck.

"Nobody will find you until it's too late to
declare. Then I might come back and untie you
or I might just forget and leave the door locked.
Nobody will come looking in here. Who would
imagine that you hadn't left ages ago, especially
when I tell the steward that I saw you heading for
the Members' bar just before the race? They'll
think you've lost your nerve. They'll prosecute
you. They may even give you a suspension. So if I
don't come back and you stay here the night,
you'll have lots to think about – like how you're
going to miss the National and watch The Black
romp home in the lead."

"It will never work!" I spat out.

"Oh, I think it already has." He looked exag-
geratedly at his watch. "Ten minutes to get to the
weighing scales. Not great odds, if you don't mind
me saying. Now, one final touch." He reached in
his pocket and pulled out some sticky tape which
he slammed across my mouth. "I'm sure you'll
work out the best thing to do about Saturday.
Because, you see, if there's a next time, I might not
be so gentle."

He turned the lights off and clicked the door
shut, locking it behind him. I was left in darkness.
I thought about tipping the chair on to the floor

but there was no one around to hear the crash and I might have to lie on the floor for hours. My whole body ached but my head worst of all. It felt as if it had stopped bleeding but the dull throb was relentless. Waves of hysteria kept rising inside me like bile. All I could think about was Dougie Barnes out there ruining my reputation, casting aspersions on my character. What if they made an example of me and doled out a suspension? What if I missed Saturday? I tried to pull myself up but the chair was too heavy and the cord dug in deeper with the tension. There was no way I could untie it. Dougie had really thought this one out. He must be laughing his head off. I began to despair.

Dry sobs were starting to rack my body when I heard footsteps along the short passage towards the door. Somebody was there. For a second, I thought it was Barnes returning. I felt like I wanted to die. Then the door handle turned and Rory called, "Justina, are you in there?"

I flipped the chair over then, bruising the side of my face. But I didn't care, didn't even feel it. I heard him pound the door with his shoulder, heard the wood splinter and then he was leaning over me, staring in disbelief, reaching into his coat pocket for the keyring penknife I'd given him out of a Christmas cracker. Tension flooded out of me and tears spurted down my nose. When he gently eased off the tape, wincing if he thought it hurt me, I couldn't help making whimpering noises. The cord fell loose and I flung my arms round his neck with almost violent desperation.

"Steady now, there, there, it's all right." He squeezed me as hard as anything. The shock of finding me like this was written all over his face. He looked devastated, and angry beyond words. It was some time before either of us could speak.

"It was Barnes, wasn't it?" he asked me gently, once I'd finally stopped trembling.

I nodded. "How did you know?"

"Ben Le Sueur rang my mobile straight after I'd spoken to you. He'd heard from Eddy Newton that you were riding and was worried about Barnes. I got the gist of what was going on from him and turned round and tore straight back up the country. Oh my God, Justina, why didn't you tell me?"

He ran his hand gently over my hair and I winced as his fingers found the blood. "What's that pig done to you?"

"Nothing, I'm fine. I just fell. It's nothing." Suddenly the time and the place came rushing back into focus. "Where's my hat?" I rasped, staggering slightly as I tried to stand for the first time. "I've got to ride! I've got to weigh in."

Horror registered on Rory's face. "You are kidding?"

"Don't you believe it, I'd rather die than give Dougie Barnes the pleasure of ruining my life." I reached for my breeches and top, pulling at my clothes. "Don't just stand there, help me!" I was running on pure adrenaline. Rory awkwardly tugged the breeches over my calves. "I shouldn't be doing this . . ."

"Rory, this is no time to play the gentleman. How long have I got?"

"You're thirty seconds over. At least let me bathe your head."

"No time. Nobody will see it under my hat anyway. I'm out of here."

"I can't let you do this. You could be concussed, you've just been—"

"Rory, I'm riding." I pecked him on the cheek and stepped into the cold air, feeling as if my legs were candyfloss instead of muscle and sinew.

Somehow, without even being aware of it, I steered Doogle Don home to victory. The buzz it gave me to imagine Dougie Barnes's face was priceless, but I was also aware that I'd made a fool of him and he wouldn't be forgiving. Now I was in even more danger.

Rory wouldn't leave my side for a second and after the prize-giving he kept one arm firmly round my waist and guided me back to his car, where Poppy was squeezed into the back seat with her head out of an open window. It was a good job he was supporting me because my legs didn't feel as if they could. I just wanted to sink into the grass and fall asleep.

I felt a lump like a tennis ball in my throat. I ruffled Poppy's ears and let her stick a spade-sized paw on my shoulder and lick the back of my right ear. "It's like having a hundred and one Dalmatians crammed in the car." I could have sworn she'd grown even more since I'd last seen her.

"I'm taking you home and then calling out the doctor. You need plenty of rest and, looking at you, a decent meal. We'll then think about speaking to the police. See what the Guv says."

"No!" I screeched in horror. "Rory promise me – no! I can't do anything to risk not riding."

"Look at yourself!" Rory swivelled the interior mirror round, and I had to acknowledge that the wan, exhausted face staring back was mine.

"I don't care. We can't tell anybody. I have to line up at the start on Saturday. I can't let Murphy down."

"And do you think a horse knows whether he's got a big race or not? All he's interested in is whether he gets his grub and his haynet's full."

"That's not true. Murphy's different. He understands. He want to prove himself as much as I do. He wants to win this race."

"Give me strength!" Rory gave a weak laugh.

"And look at these wrists." He tenderly turned over my hands to reveal the vicious bruises forming under the skin. "Should the person who did this be allowed to get away with it?"

"Of course not." I snatched my hands back. "But now's not the time to create a fuss. Besides, there's something else I've got to do."

"Enlighten me." He raised an eyebrow enquiringly.

I fished in my changing bag for the slip of paper on which was written the information I'd managed to prise from Badger. An address for Melody Phipps at Ivydown Stables in Southport.

"It's going to take a while to explain, so if you just start driving – " I coughed nervously, trying to find the right words. "The thing is – basically – I've got to go to Southport. It would be much easier if you'd agree to come with me. I think that the motorway is that way ... You'd better put your indicator on now ..."

Seven

As it was, we didn't set off until the following morning. Rory took me home and tucked me up on the settee in a blanket and fed me chicken soup followed by warm pitta bread with jam. Poppy rested her huge head in the crook of my elbow and watched over me with worried eyes. I was alarmed by how exhausted I felt. I could barely lift an arm without thinking I needed a crane to help me. Rory quietly got on with administering aspirin and gently cleaned the blood from my hair using Animalintex poultice because we'd run out of cotton wool. Luckily, Mandy was out at a hen night so there was no need for explanations.

We watched the Grand National preview which always went out on the Wednesday night before the race. Two other horses and last year's winner were on first. Mark interviewed the jockeys and trainers and then it switched to some film of The Black scorching up an all-weather track and leaping a huge birch fence. My stomach tensed into knots as I leaned forward, my eyes glued to the set.

"Sit down!" I screeched at Rory as he went into the kitchen to fetch a beer, making the picture go fuzzy. If you didn't sit as quiet as a mouse when the television was on, the aerial went on the blink. Dougie Barnes flashed on to the screen, all smug and confident and I felt a light fade inside me. It was hard enough to ride round the Grand National without having to face a thug like him – how could I hold my nerve when he had scared me so badly?

The Black circled and walked back to the camera on a loose rein.

I watched closely. How a horse walked often determined how it galloped. The Black stretched out with long, easy strides and a powerhouse behind. I had to admit he was an athlete of a horse.

"He's a stallion," Rory said in surprise. "He won't be wanting to touch any of his fences, that's for sure."

I shot him a quizzical look.

"Use your imagination," he said, raising his eyebrows.

The next bit cut straight to Murphy, flying over the mock-up Canal Turn fence and galloping as if his hooves were on fire. I squirmed at seeing myself ride but then got caught up in the excitement of what we were doing. There was a frenzy of energy, a purpose and a united goal which came across from the very first shot. The Guv'nor was shown, barking instructions, striding across the turf with a grizzling Chelsea under one arm, wanting better and better each time. It was gripping viewing. Even Rory stayed absolutely still, spellbound by the flying horse and young girl working to achieve perfect jumping of one of the most difficult Grand National fences.

Afterwards I sat in silence, feeling the magic and mentally rehearsing what would happen over the next few days.

"Will you be all right tonight?" Rory surveyed me with worried eyes, the soft, dark irises and black lashes which I'd first fallen for full of tenderness. "Are you absolutely sure you want to see this Melody Phipps rather than just speaking to her on the phone? It could be a waste of time, the journey, I mean. She won't want to rake up old memories, not if she's in a wheelchair."

"I need to see her," I answered in measured tones. I couldn't describe why. It was more than just encouraging her to speak up against Barnes. It was all to do with comradeship and being on the same side. She knew how I felt – she'd been there. She could give me more valuable advice for Saturday's race than anyone. And hopefully I could give her something too, even if it was only inspiration to succeed.

Rory lingered over a gentle kiss. "I never want to see you hurt like that again."

"You won't have to," I grinned. "From now on it's mixed changing rooms or nothing at all. I quite missed the lads, even their stupid jokes. Goodnight, Sir Lancelot and sleep tight." I pecked him on the cheek and then hugged him close. "Thanks," I whispered, meaning it. "I'll see you at dawn."

We crept down the drive at five-thirty the next morning, before anybody was up and about.

"You realize the Guv'nor will go ballistic when he finds out that both his stable jockeys have done a bunk?" Rory swung the steering wheel and passed me the road atlas.

"He's got no idea that Barnes has been threatening me since the fall at the racecourse. He'd be hurt if he knew I hadn't turned to him."

"I don't blame you for not. It would be like approaching a man-eating crocodile with a white handkerchief!"

"He isn't that bad," I laughed. "I just don't want him pulling me out of the race. Regardless of what everyone thinks, he really does care and he'd rather I didn't race than risk getting hurt."

Three toilet stops and one petrol stop later we

crossed into Lancashire. We were still miles from Southport.

"I never realized Liverpool was so far." I tried to hide my discomfort by sucking a lemon bomb very loudly. Rory was used to driving long distances and hardly seemed to notice, which was a blessing because, unbeknown to him, I hadn't checked that Melody would be in or that she was still living at the same address.

"Isn't Southport where they used to train Red Rum?" Rory broke the silence.

I couldn't believe he even had to ask. Everybody knows that Red Rum trained on the Southport beach and that it was the sea which healed his leg injury and made him into a superstar racehorse, with a little help from his trainer Ginger McCain.

"Well, sorry for speaking out of turn but I'm not a walking encyclopaedia on the Rummy phenomenon," he said good-naturedly after I'd finished exclaiming at his ignorance.

"Legend," I corrected, going glassy-eyed just thinking about my hero.

"If you've dragged me up here just to have a look at where he used to dig and poo in the sand, I'll clip your ears and your backside."

"And I'll have you show a little respect," I sniffed, laughing.

I'd spent most of our relationship talking about Murphy or Red Rum or Desert Orchid. He must know their blood groups and hoof prints by now. I offered him a lemon bomb on the palm of my hand, like you would offer a treat to a horse.

"I'll take that as an apology," he grinned.

"Here, turn now, now! Turn!"

Ivydown Stables was a large Victorian house surrounded by cedar trees. We couldn't see any stables from the front of the drive. Nervous now that we'd finally arrived, I hovered by the car door waiting for Rory to make the first move.

Every footstep seemed to reverberate in the still, cold air. The place had a deserted feeling. I wanted to groan out loud at the thought that nobody was home. Rory looked agitated and jangled his car keys. We were both feeling tense.

"Can I help you?" A voice called from a gap in the hedge. Startled, I spun round to see a woman manoeuvring a wheelchair across the lawn and up a specially built ramp.

I took in the blonde hair tied back in a ponytail and the delicate, pretty face. The full force of what Dougie Barnes had done hit me like a steel girder across the ribs. I found it difficult to catch my breath. As she wheeled closer, recognition flitted across her features. She had probably watched the preview last night, but couldn't believe I was standing in front of her. She held out her hand and her mouth quivered into an uncertain smile.

"Justina Brooks and Rory Calligan," I mumbled, embarrassed by being recognized. I shook her hand and then Rory did as well.

She looked momentarily stunned before showing us into the house. Immediately I was enchanted by a tiny Shetland pony standing in the kitchen eating an apple from a mat on the floor.

"Oh, don't mind Chutney. It's more effort keeping him out than letting him in. He likes to watch television. His favourite programmes are *Blue Peter* and *Coronation Street*." She rubbed the little skewbald face affectionately and then two Siamese cats and a pack of dogs flung themselves through the opposite door followed by another woman who was the spitting image of Melody.

"Mum, you'll never guess who's here!" Melody was obviously excited, but there was a nervous edge to her voice that was impossible to miss.

Mrs Phipps was clearly used to taking charge and in no time had the kettle on and was setting out an array of home-made cakes and biscuits. "Just push Chutney out of the way. Dogs – baskets, now!" Two terriers and three spaniels slunk under the table for about half a minute. I caught Melody gazing at Rory and filled with pride.

"I've been following Murphy on the television. He's got amazing scope. It's incredible what you've achieved. I should think every horse-mad girl in the country would just love to be you."

I squirmed with embarrassment, aware of how Barnes had forced her to relinquish her dreams and confined her to a wheelchair. I caught Rory's eye. We both knew that this was the perfect moment. I put my cup down carefully in its saucer. "I came here because I need your help. It's connected with Dougie Barnes . . ."

The name seemed to send a chill right through the room. Mrs Phipps stopped clattering at the sink. Melody sat as still as a statue, only a rapid swallowing showing that she'd heard me.

"I'm sorry, I should never have come – I really didn't want to upset you." I half stood, feeling terrible. She had suffered enough. It was obviously a subject about which she didn't want to speak. "Please, forgive me."

"No, sit down." Mrs Phipps waved her hand towards the chair. "I've told Melody a thousand times that she can't move on with her life until she faces up to the past. It's no good burying it and thinking that's the end of it. We have to live with the consequences every day."

I glanced across at Melody. Her cheeks were flushed. "I didn't ever think he'd start riding again," she said quietly. "For eight years we've lived without mentioning that man's name. Now

76

every time we switch on the telly he pops up like a curse."

Mrs Phipps went across to her daughter and held her shoulders. "We did wonder if he was harassing you or whether he'd turned over a new leaf."

"He's scaring the wits out of me," I said honestly. "I'm terrified that he might try something on Saturday, but if I go to the Jockey Club they're going to just think it's sour grapes and I'm trying it on. I have absolutely no proof and none of the other jockeys will come forward to back me up. I was hoping Melody might be able to tell her story to give mine credence."

"I'm sorry." Melody pushed her chair away from the table "I can't do it." Her face creased with anguish and fear. "If he found out, if he came after me again."

"But he's dangerous," I pleaded. "You can't let him get away with it. Nor can I."

"Well, you'll have to deal with it yourself. You're stronger than I am, and you're not confined to this contraption." Her voice was soaked in bitterness.

"Help me – and it will help you," I tried one last time, but she was shaking her head so violently a hair slide fell out.

Rory touched my arm.

"I'm sorry." I stood up to leave.

Mrs Phipps followed us to the front door.

"If I can get her to change her mind . . ." Her voice trailed off. I could only imagine the hurt and anguish that Dougie Barnes had caused this family. "Good luck for Aintree, although our Mel always says it's not good luck, it's good jockey."

"I'll try my best."

"So what now?" Rory switched on the car engine. "A motorway café burger or a walk on Southport beach?"

I felt exhausted and deflated as I turned the key in the back door just as it was getting dark. I didn't dare go round to the main yard because Scooby or Mandy would have had to cover for me and I'd probably get thrown in the water trough or buried alive in the muck heap.

As soon as I walked into the kitchen, before I'd even turned on the light, I sensed a difference. A zingy waft of lemon mixed with furniture polish hit my nostrils full on. Rory reached past me and switched on the light. The kitchen was gleaming. There wasn't a dirty pot in sight. We even had a new teacloth, and a pair of yellow Marigold gloves balanced over the taps. There was a note on the top of the fridge. "Don't say I don't keep my word. But that's the first and last time I tackle your drains."

A message flashed on the answering machine. I

suddenly had a feeling of foreboding. I pressed the button and closed my eyes.

"Justina, how could you do this to your brothers? They were so excited about seeing you, and to just go out for the day. It's their birthday – they're five years old. I have to say I'm disappointed in you as a daughter. If this is what being a jockey has done to you. What's happened to that caring, selfless girl? I can't believe you'd treat your family like this."

Even on the tape I could hear the hurt behind her anger. I switched it off, feeling devastated. The presents and balloons and party poppers were stacked under the stairs. How could I have forgotten? I loved my baby brothers, more than anything.

"It's all right, you'll make it up to them." Rory wrapped his arms round my shoulders.

"No it's not," I gulped. "It's unforgivable. Am I so caught up in myself that I can't remember my twin brothers' birthday?"

Rory didn't get a chance to answer. There was a heavy pounding at the door.

"It's Badger." Rory reached for the handle.

"If you don't mind me interrupting, there's something important I've got to say." Badger stood in the little porch holding his cap. "I think you both ought to get yourselves down to the hospital. It's the Guv, you see. He's had a stroke."

Eight

"He's had a TIA – transient ischaemic attack." The nurse looked directly at Rory. "I presume you've contacted any relatives?"

"What does that mean?" I almost shouted, feeling self-control slide away.

"He's had a very mild stroke, but there's no need to be alarmed. It hasn't had any lasting effect."

I felt the room rotate slightly and black dots dance in front of my eyes. My granny had had a stroke a few years ago and it killed her. "Can I see him?" My voice sounded as if it belonged to someone else and my mouth felt as if it was made of papier mâché. The nurse led us briskly down the corridor to Dixon Ward.

"We're only keeping him in overnight for observation. He'll be able to go home tomorrow."

"But what if he has another one?" My voice rose.

"Well, of course there's always that possibility,

but Mr Brown understands that he's got to have a major change of lifestyle."

"But he trains ninety racehorses!"

The nurse pursed her lips. There was no need to say any more. And the reality of what had happened hit me like a sledgehammer. The Guv'nor was ill. It was unthinkable.

"He's in the third bed along." The nurse left us to tend to another patient. Tears sprang to my eyes as I saw the Guv'nor, suddenly looking very small and old, lying in a hospital bed.

"Darnation, what do these people think they're playing at?" He growled, thumping the meal tray which was balanced over the bed and spilling jelly and custard everywhere. "Rory, find a doctor. I can't spend a minute longer in here. Don't they understand I've got a business to run?" He didn't sound like a man who understood that he had to have a major change of lifestyle.

"I didn't bring any grapes," I mumbled. "But you might like these." I pulled his form books and the *Racing Post* out of a carrier bag. I'd stopped at his office to collect them before coming to the hospital.

"That's more like it," he grumbled. "But I don't suppose you remembered my pipe and that bottle of claret in the office?"

"Guv, I don't think you're supposed—"

He gave me a look which would fry eyebrows.

"All right, I'll bring them in later."

"Do you know they won't let you use mobile phones in these places?" He snorted and pulled a moth-eaten, ruby velvet jacket round his thin shoulders. "Where's Rory? Tell him to ask for my shirt and trousers which they've taken off to some hidden place."

In the next bed, an elderly man holding an oxygen mask to his mouth surveyed the Guv'nor with obvious fascination. I had to turn away to hide a smile. The Guv'nor sounded as though he was in the stable yard, not a hospital ward. He couldn't be that ill if he was taking over.

Rory came back into the ward towards us. I could tell by the way he was walking that it was bad news. His body language spoke reluctance and awkwardness. "The nurse was mistaken when she said you were only here for observation. Apparently they want to run more tests," he started in a dry voice. "You'll have to stay here tonight, and maybe tomorrow night as well."

We both held out breath, expecting the Guv'nor to explode. Instead he flopped back against the pillow and seemed to give up. The fighting spirit, always so clear in the hard, craggy lines of his face, vanished. Almost instantly, he was like the other patients in the ward – vulnerable-looking and unsure and scared.

I glanced sharply at Rory and knew that he

could see it too. Immediately my heart started beating faster. What if he died? What if he wasn't there to see me win the Grand National? I couldn't do without him. I thought of the past two years and how much the Guv'nor had helped me. I would never have made it as a jockey without his belief and support. I couldn't imagine a world without him. He was the force that kept me sane, helping me and guiding me and believing in me.

"I haven't gone yet." The Guv'nor opened one eye as if he could read my thoughts. "Rory, pull the curtain round the bed so I can have a private word with you both."

Rory did as he was told, embarrassed because the other patients were watching with interest. I scraped my chair closer to the bed. Rory looked nervous, like a child expected to be told off. The Guv'nor propped himself up on the pillows and a touch of colour came back into his cheeks. Then, in a whisper, he dropped his bombshell. "I want you to take Murphy away from Dolphin Barn and hide him. He's not safe there."

My jaw dropped. "What's happening, Guv? Are you serious?"

"Yes, I am. Badger swears he saw someone late last night snooping around the yard. It could have been one of the lads, or anybody, I don't know, but when Badger challenged him, he disappeared. Stuck in here, I can't protect Murphy's Law but

I'm darned if I'm going to let my best racehorse be got at before Saturday, not when he stands the best chance I've had of winning since Dolphin twenty years ago."

"But where would we go?" I breathed, struggling to absorb what the Guv'nor was asking.

"Rory will think of something. But you mustn't tell a soul where you go. Not even Badger. Just take the horsebox and go. Nobody must know your whereabouts. No one. Is that clear?"

I nodded vigorously. I felt sick at the thought of anything happening to Murphy. He'd been threatened before and survived it. I wouldn't see him hurt again. My thoughts immediately turned towards Barnes. If he couldn't scare me off, would he go for my horse instead? It was possible. When it came to the Grand National I knew anything was possible. It was the richest prize in racing and some people would stop at nothing to win.

"I'll meet you on the morning of the race at the track," the Guv'nor was saying. I could see the energy running out of him, the drawn face growing paler again. "Remember, Murphy needs his pipe opener before the race. He needs a solid run to warm him up, get him going well. Don't ring me. Someone might have bugged the phones and be able to trace the call. We'll need to walk the course together though, before the race. There's so much I've got to tell you." He broke off, gasping for breath and I realized that he must have been feeling ill for a long time.

"Just make sure you're there," I squeezed his gnarled hand. "No mad parties and swinging off the chandeliers." I tried to make light, but my face was set rigid. If I relaxed a muscle I'd burst into tears.

"Go on, get out of here." He shook off my hand and waved me away.

We slipped through the curtain and walked down the ward past the food trolley. "God, I hope the old buzzard makes it," Rory whispered.

I realized then that the Guv'nor was fighting his own personal battle every bit as arduous as the Grand National. "He's not lost a race yet," I answered. "Not one that really matters."

"Justina, wake up!" Rory had let himself into the cottage and was shaking me awake. I'd just been dreaming about my brothers and buying them a whole toyshop which they didn't want. I hadn't had a chance to phone them yet to explain what had happened. "Justina, we're leaving! Now!" Rory ruffled my hair. I sat up, barely awake, and started struggling into crumpled jeans.

"What time is it?"

"Four. Keep your voice down. We don't want to wake Mandy."

"Why are we leaving so early?" I hunted for socks.

"So we don't have to answer a whole load of questions. Now hurry up. I'll be outside."

"Where are we going?"

"I'll tell you later."

I picked up a bag that I had packed the night before and groped my way down the narrow stairs. In the stable yard, the horsebox was backed up, ready to set off down the drive. Rain was slanting down. A light was on in Murphy's stable and the security lights in the yard had come on. It was alarming that not one of the lads in the hostel had woken up. No wonder the Guv'nor had been worried.

Badger was inside the stable bandaging Murphy's tail. Murphy wickered excitedly at seeing me and strained against the rope. "That should do him." Badger walked round his near side and ran a hand expertly under the layers of rugs. "You'll need to check him regularly on the journey, wherever you're going." The resentment in his voice was impossible to miss.

"I'll be travelling with him."

"Right, that's everything then. I can't say I agree with it, but good luck for Saturday. I think you'll need it." He ducked back into the stable.

I released the slipknot securing Murphy and led him out over the cobbles to Rory and the waiting box. A shiver of excitement rippled down my spine. We were stepping into the unknown. It was phase one of the adventure ahead. Murphy thundered up the ramp, keen to get out of the rain. Next time he saw Dolphin Barn, he'd be a Grand National runner and possibly a champion. The whole of Cheltenham might turn out to see him.

I jumped nimbly into the living quarters of the horsebox which led through a tiny door to the horses. From there I could walk easily through to the cab and Rory. Through the side mirror I could see some of the stable lads spilling out of the hostel. Too late, lads, you'll have to get the story from Badger.

"This feels like being on the run," I shouted to Rory as we drove out of the yard. "Where are we going?"

"Well, you know our little chat about Southport beach and what it did for Red Rum? Let's just say, Murphy will be treading the same sand dunes."

"Melody Phipps! Perfect!" I shouted, starting to relax for the first time in weeks. And it *was* perfect. I had a really good feeling.

"We'll have to turn back!" I yelled through to the cab ten miles later. A thought had hit me like a bolt in the back of the neck. "We've forgotten Gertie. He'll go crazy in his stable, you know how he needs company." I had bought Murphy cheap from a sale because he was what is known as a box walker. In other words, he used to run round and round his stable, burning off weight and exhausting himself, all because he hated being alone. Stabling Gertie with him had cured him of that but I couldn't take the risk that he might revert back, especially so close to the biggest race of his life, especially if he was going to be in a strange stable for the next couple of days.

"Forget it," Rory shouted. We were coming off the slip road to join the motorway. Cars roared past in a never-ending stream. "We're supposed to be keeping a low profile. Don't you think having a goat tagging along is going to give us away? We might as well stick a flashing beacon on top of Murphy's head. I'll sleep with him if it comes to it. He can't snore any louder than some of the lads I have to share with when I'm away racing."

"I'll do it!" I volunteered.

"You'll do no such thing. It's early nights and plenty of sleep. You look like death, as it is."

"Gee, you know how to make a girl feel beautiful," I chuckled. Rory was even more gorgeous when he was being masterful. I didn't argue with him. The truth was that I felt tired from my bones outwards. I needed to build up my strength.

The rain had stopped and the sun was fighting through when we turned into Ivydown Livery Stables. Both Mrs Phipps and Melody were waiting in the gravelled yard with a stable open. Mrs Phipps had told Rory it was the least they could do for us in the circumstances. As Murphy danced down the ramp there was a noticeable difference in Melody. Her cheeks were full of colour and a sparkle lit her eyes.

"It's the first time she's seen a racehorse since the accident," Mrs Phipps whispered. "This will do more good than any doctor or specialist. She's already turned a corner."

There didn't seem to be any other people or horses around and it crossed my mind that Ivydown wasn't exactly a thriving business. Murphy settled into his new stable without any sign that he was going to start box walking. He immediately teamed up with Chutney, the Shetland pony who seemed to make as good a companion as Gertie.

I could practically taste the tangy sea air. Tomorrow, Murphy would start his last piece of serious work on the beach on which Red Rum had raced.

"Run, run run!" I pushed my hands forwards up the powerful neck. A spray of sea water enveloped us. I couldn't see for a few seconds, just taste salt on my lips and feel stinging in the corners of my eyes. The wind howled along the sand, driving Murphy on like a horse possessed. We were flying along the edge of the water where it was four to five inches deep. Rory had borrowed the Phipps's four-wheel drive and was further up on the hard sand alongside, setting the pace. Murphy was cruising along at thirty miles an hour, defying anything to beat him. He was relishing the beach, the change of scene, the sunshine, the water under his hooves.

Seagulls circled above, tossed and buffeted in the wind. The tide pushed further in, lapping and dragging at Murphy's legs. But nothing could stop us, we were both doing what we were born to do. Race. As a team. Horse and rider as one. There was something spiritual about the moment, and if I closed my eyes and concentrated, I could see a bay horse alongside us, urging Murphy on, galloping and bucking for the pure joy of it. I was sure that Red Rum's spirit was with us, and I would carry that belief for ever.

"Whoa, boy, whoa, steady now." I locked my feet forward and bridged the reins, pulling up before the soft beach sand turned into mud and stones at the end. Rory stopped his vehicle and ran across to us. The wind was gusting now, tugging at Murphy's quarter sheet which was vital to keep his muscles warm. I turned a circle, calming him down, getting his mind to settle. Steam rose from his back and every vein in his neck stood out because he was ready to spring away again as soon as I relaxed my fingers on the reins.

"That was brilliant." Rory came close, clearly impressed. "Time to play in the sea."

Murphy loved it. He pawed at the water, spun around, squealed, half-reared. He splashed up to his belly in the ice-cold water and nipped my foot when I shrieked at the temperature. We both came out wet through even though I'd been on his back. To finish off we took him up to the sand dune and let him kick and dig, and finally roll without his saddle.

"This is doing him so much good," I shivered, wrapping myself in Rory's coat.

"You realize you'll spend the rest of the morning brushing sand out of his coat?"

"I don't care. It's worth it to see him so happy." I beamed at my superstar racehorse as he lay down for a fourth roll in the golden sand and the sunshine.

"Come on," Rory put an arm round my shoulders. "We'd better get back to the horsebox. We can't afford to be seen."

"The Guv's on his way up the motorway with Scooby and Badger. Apparently he's being more cantankerous than ever, though he does claim that he's got one of the nurses' phone numbers. Oh and he's had a word with your mum and dad and they're on their way to Aintree as we speak, with your brothers." Rory was leaning over the stable door, his mobile phone in his hand.

Relief washed away the guilt and worry which had been building up inside me. I slowly wound the bandages high up round Murphy's legs, each of which must be worth the equivalent of a Premiership footballer's. We were getting ready for Aintree. Murphy sensed the occasion and started hopping from one hoof to the other. An unexpected wave of nerves crashed in my stomach. Only twenty-three hours to go.

It had been reported on the morning news that Murphy was in hiding, and that he was rumoured to be quite close to Aintree. We didn't know how they'd found out, but it added to the excitement. Three girls had been shown wearing Murphy sweat-shirts and waving a banner and the reporter talked about how Murphy's Law and his young, female jockey had captured the hearts of the nation. Well over 800,000 people in Britain alone were expected to tune in to the race at three forty-five tomorrow. Facts like that I could do without knowing.

Mrs Phipps peered over the stable door,

obviously saddened that Murphy was leaving. "Where's Melody?" I asked.

"She's gone to London for the day for an appointment, but she'll be back for the race tomorrow. She asked me to give you this." She passed me a small jewellery box and inside, on a red background, lay a beautiful diamond clasp.

"It's for your stock," Mrs Phipps went on. "To wear during the race."

There was a note which I quickly unfolded.

Dear Justina

You have been an inspiration to me and the whole country with your courage and determination. I would like you to have this diamond stock-pin to bring you luck during the race. Your example has given me the confidence to set up a business bringing on racehorse foals and yearlings. If you wonder where I am today, I have travelled to the Jockey Club headquarters in Portman Square to make a complaint against Dougie Barnes. I doubt it will be enough for them to take action, but at least they will be alerted to the kind of man he is. Who knows, maybe it will even frighten him off making any further attacks. Go out there tomorrow and whip the pants off him. We're all with you, every step of the way. You have a great horse and an amazing talent. I'm sure you will both go down in history.

You can do it, Justina!

Melody

I smiled at Mrs Phipps, my eyes full of tears. I couldn't find words to thank her or Melody.

"We really ought to be going," Rory urged, looking pointedly at his watch. "It's a bit like being best man at a wedding," he apologized to Mrs Phipps.

"Go, go!" Mrs Phipps waved her arms as if she was shooing chickens.

We sprang into action.

"Tell Melody I'll win for her," I shouted through the cab window as we were leaving. I was clutching the diamond pin. "Thanks for everything!"

"See you in the winner's enclosure!" Mrs Phipps shouted back as the horsebox pulled away down the drive, crunching gravel.

I leaned back inside the cab and closed my eyes. We were on the final leg of the journey. To Aintree. At last!

Nine

It was two o'clock in the morning. Streetlights glinted orange in the road below. I couldn't sleep. I heard people in the hotel coming back to their rooms after a night out. Some of the jockeys would still be in the bar. Everywhere there was a pre-National buzz.

I tossed and turned. Three o'clock. Still awake. I switched on the beside light then switched it off again. The room felt hot and stuffy. I lay there, wishing desperately that I had stood up to Rory and slept in the horsebox. I rode the course over and over in my mind. I couldn't afford to make a mistake. So many people were relying on me . . .

I must have slept because I was suddenly woken by my alarm clock.

Six a.m. Grand National morning. I reached out, pulled back the curtains and gasped. Everywhere was covered in snow.

I tried to stay calm. The soft, white blanket touched everything. People were getting into cars, wiping the soft flakes off windscreens and bonnets. They were moving, walking along the street. It wasn't too deep. It didn't mean the National would be cancelled.

The phone rang, making me jump. It was the Guv'nor. "Justina, what are you waiting for? Room service? Get yourself down to reception before you put me back in hospital. You've got thirty seconds." He barked down the phone in his usual fashion. Normality returned to an upended world. The Guv'nor was back on form.

I raced down the stairs, in too much of a hurry to wait for the lift. On each floor excited people were scurrying along with binoculars and picnic hampers, race cards and fold-up seats. The snow hadn't dampened the atmosphere. The electric charge was phenomenal and we weren't even at the racecourse yet.

"Don't worry, it's thawing already." The Guv'nor read my thoughts. We were sitting at breakfast and I didn't think either of us could have faced it if the race had been cancelled. We'd worked too hard, put too much on the line. Emotionally we had bottomed out. "But the going will be heavier than an Irish bog. Anybody who sets a hot pace will be on their knees by the second circuit." The concern in the Guv'nor's voice sent a shiver down my spine. "You'll have to hold him up. No good haring off. Hold him back, make sure he never gets more than two lengths ahead of the other runners."

Short of hobbling him I wondered how the Guv'nor thought I'd achieve that but I didn't say anything. Instead I swallowed my coffee, knowing I needed a caffeine injection.

"Full English breakfast?" A waitress hovered with what looked like enough food to feed an army. The Guv'nor gestured at me.

"I don't think so," I mumbled, panic-stricken, as the waitress put the plate down in front of me.

"You need strength," the Guv'nor barked, pinching my arm as if it were a chicken leg.

"I'm surprised you're not feeding me spinach," I grumbled, sticking my fork tentatively into a sausage.

"Banjo Boy can run in the mud. If he doesn't fall, he'll be a threat. You know Ben Le Sueur's stable colours – watch him – he's on a one-pace horse but he has bags of stamina. Don't let him get a lead." The Guv'nor was tapping the table with a knife in agitation. "We don't know about The Black but at the security stables this morning he looked one tough cookie. I bet he'll dig in deep and find a turn of foot."

I looked at him in awe. He was planning the race like a military operation. Nobody would even suspect that he had just come out of hospital. It was only six-thirty in the morning now. What time had he been prowling around, weighing up the opposition? Security was so tight on the course that nobody could enter the stable area unless they had a pass or were escorted by a trainer. A swarm of butterflies fluttered in my stomach. I picked up my coffee cup with both hands so that the Guv'nor wouldn't notice that I was trembling. Nerves, to him, were a sign of weakness.

"Gee, I know who you are!" A waitress carrying a tray full of Danish pastries put one hand on my shoulder. "You're that jockey who's going to ride in the National. Oh, honey, you're so dainty. It's gotta be a publicity stunt. If I was your mother I wouldn't let you near that course."

She moved on and I could swear she'd heard the Guv'nor gnashing his teeth. I pressed my top lip over my bottom one to smother a laugh, but deep down she'd struck a nerve. What was my mother feeling now? I was her little girl but I was about to endure one of the toughest physical tests that the world of racing had to offer.

"I need to see Mum and Dad," I blurted out. "Before the race."

"Of course." The Guv'nor seemed to understand. "We'll leave now, but not by the main entrance. They've got green curtains and carpet and I'm not taking any risks." He never walked past green on a race day if he could help it. Today superstition would be running rife.

I quickly found out that preparation for the Grand National was steeped in tradition. The jockeys always rode the horses round the course early on the morning race, for example. Today I would be with them.

The thought of riding out on the hallowed turf was overwhelming. I couldn't speak as I looked down the long line of thirty-seven runners being prepared for morning exercise. Jockeys, stable lads and lasses, trainers and owners mingled in a frenzy of activity, checking horses and tack and exchanging advice. The atmosphere was electric.

"Justina!"

I looked around wildly, suddenly realizing that the Guv'nor wasn't at my side. He was leaning against a wall, bent over double, gasping for breath.

"Guv!" I rushed forward to hold one of his elbows. Suddenly I realized that he wasn't better at all. It was all an act. He was drawing on grit and courage just to remain upright.

"Keep your voice down. I can stand, I'm all right. Pass me that stick." He flicked a hand towards his walking stick, which was lying on a melting patch of snow.

I stooped down quickly and whisked it up. "Guv . . ."

"Enough. Murphy is the one who counts." He looked dreadful. "Let's get on."

"He's got more ginger in him than a cake factory. Nothing will keep him down." Scooby banged the currycomb clean and stood back from his charge, bursting with pride. Murphy looked sensational. His red coat gleamed like polished wood. He strained against the leadrope and pawed impatiently at the shavings. Scooby was right. He was bang on form.

The Guv'nor ran his hands down Murphy's slender, iron-hard legs and across his back to the croup. "Right, let's get some tack on him. I want a walk, trot and canter up the straight, nothing too strenuous."

The ground squelched, leaving a sodden imprint with every stride. Murphy chucked up his head, impatient and confused that I wasn't urging him on. All the horses were either jack-knifing sideways or fly bucking as they trotted down the rails. Racecourses were for racing, not for exercise, so it was no wonder they were fretting and boiling over.

A quarter sheet slipped round the belly of a grey horse, causing it to buck, throwing its jockey. A small group near the start circled at a walk and I headed in that direction, hardly daring to look across the famous spruce fences. That would come later.

Suddenly, without warning, heavy hoofbeats thundered up behind me. The brush of a horse passing too close caused Murphy to swerve and whip round. I had to fight to cling on as Murphy reared up high and straight. He was exploding with energy and the other horse had set him off. It was exactly what the Guv'nor didn't want.

"Think you're clever, do you, pulling in your Barbie friends and getting them to tell tales to the stewards?"

The voice was unmistakable. I shortened my reins and turned a frothing Murphy to face Dougie Barnes.

He crouched in the saddle of The Black, keeping the horse straight with his whip. The fury in his face distorted his features. He'd obviously had a severe warning from official quarters.

"It won't do you any good anyway. When you line up in front of that tape do you really think you've got what it takes? You're going to let down everyone – not just your connections, but the whole country, everyone who is piling money on your back, believing in a stupid fairy tale. You're going to get what's coming to you." He sliced the whip down The Black's flank forcing him from a walk straight into a gallop. Murphy spun round and half reared, demented that I wouldn't let him race.

Even now, even when he knew the stewards were on to him, Barnes knew how to cause trouble, to stick the knife in. Murphy was lathered in sweat, jumpy as a spring and losing precious energy. I had to calm him down, steady his nerves before he wore himself ragged.

We jogged in an uncontrolled sideways motion, but as I tried to soothe him I couldn't stop shaking myself. No matter how I tried to fight it, Dougie Barnes had sown the seeds of doubt. How could someone like me ever get round the Grand National course, let alone win it?

"Line up on the outside. Don't let him put a long one in at the first. Get him in a rhythm." The Guv'nor and I were walking the course. "Travel down the outer to Bechers Brook. The descent is steepest on the inside so don't drift. Sit quiet. You don't want to be pulling him about going into a fence as big as Bechers. Track back towards the inner ready for the Canal Turn. Watch out for loose horses. They're all over the place at this stage."

The Guv'nor stopped in front of each fence and assessed the ground and the take-off. He was rattling out instructions. There was so much to remember.

Walking the course, being here, breathing in the smell of spruce and bruised grass – the course came alive in a way unimaginable from the television. The jumps looked ten times bigger for a start.

Rory, the Guv'nor and I were together and we hung back from the other jockeys and trainers. They were full of jokes and banter, trying to cover up strung-out nerves. I just wanted to focus on what was ahead.

Unlike nearly everyone else, the Guv'nor insisted we walk the course twice. In his condition, with just a stick to hold him up, Rory and I thought he was mad but we didn't dare argue. Four and a half miles in heavy-going was enough for most people, never mind someone who'd just come out of hospital.

Rory tried to be supportive, but I could see the worry in his eyes. Each fence on the second circuit seemed beyond the powers of a horse. We knew the ground was against us. Murphy would hate it, every gluey, energy-sapping step. The covering of snow had all but melted, bar the odd pile of slush.

"By the time you get to the twenty-third, you'll know how much you've got left in the tank. Weigh up the other survivors."

Fence seven on the first lap, twenty-three on the second, is famously called Foinavon, after a 100-1-shot winning racehorse. He was the only horse to stay standing once when the rest of the field stopped, fell, or was brought down by the other runners. That was the kind of freakish good luck I could do with. In buckets.

Doubt clung to me but if the Guv'nor was concerned, he didn't show it. It crossed my mind that the £290,000 prize money would mean that he could retire and take things easy.

The rest of the morning and early afternoon stretched out like a blank calendar. It was time to kill, to will away. The horses were all back in their stables after a light breakfast and now had a chance to relax before the race. Of course it was easier for them because they didn't have any notion of what faced them.

Rory and the Guv'nor led the way up to one of the hospitality boxes. Even today, when I was struggling to string a sentence together, the Guv'nor was insisting that I talk to sponsors and reporters and potential owners. What was the point of refusing? I didn't have the strength. I seemed to have lost all my fighting spirit out there when faced with the Aintree fences. I took a deep breath as the door swung back.

"Dustbin!" My twin brothers, who had never been able to pronounce Justina, flew into my arms. Love and warmth surged up inside my chest until I thought I wouldn't be able to breathe. I clung to them, burying my face in their soft, curly hair and feeling their tiny arms round my neck. Mum and Dad were there too, and Grandad and Auntie Gladys and Nanny Beckett, who had looked after me while Mum and Dad were at work. Behind them were the Phippses and Mandy and a load of people from the yard. Even Badger was there, dressed in a pinstripe suit.

Sobs of gratitude welled up inside me, but I managed not to cry. Best of all, Mum came and gave me a hug and I knew that all the years of arguing were forgiven. She was behind me, lock, stock and barrel. It showed in her eyes, in the way she held her chin. I hugged Dad and everyone else and then had a sip of champagne and half an egg sandwich. But despite the happiness, my eyes never wandered far from the clock on the wall. I was watching its hands getting closer and closer to the time at which I'd have to leave the box.

Rory was at the end of the room with a finger in one ear shouting into a mobile phone. There was something in his stance which told me he had a ride. He was pushing his way across to me before he'd finished the conversation. "I'm in," he grinned, chucking the phone up in the air. "That no-hoper I went to see, the jockey's bailed out. I'll probably crash at the first but I'm in. I'm in the National! I'd better go see the trainer."

His bravery highlighted my weakness. He was about to climb on a horse for the first time and jaunt round the Grand National track. I was on the favourite and was scared witless.

"Mum, I need a word. Now – in the ladies . . ." I took her by the arm and led her in. "I can't do it! You'll have to go and tell the Guv, he's still got time to find another jockey." I was shaking uncontrollably. I felt feverish with panic. Mum stared blankly at me for a moment and then put one hand on my shoulder and the other under my chin.

"Now listen to me. You're my daughter. I know you inside out. I'll admit that when I dropped you off at that scruffy flea-infested cottage two years ago, I was appalled. I wanted you to fail and go back to your studies. But you proved me wrong. You showed guts and determination, and you worked like stink to make something of yourself. I'm more proud of you than I could possibly find words to explain. If you back out now, you'll hate yourself for the rest of your life. It's not the winning, it's the doing. If you only make one circuit, it's an achievement. You'll inspire hundreds, thousands, of young girls. How many people get the chance to do that at your age?"

"*Dark Stranger, Listen Timmy, Inis Cara, Edmond, You're Agoodun* . . ." The names rolled off the television screen. Cheers and whoops erupted from the weighing room as thirty-seven jockeys prepared for action. The background music and parade of past winners filled the room. Different aftershaves and deodorants mingled with the anticipation in the air. Even the jockeys who were usually the most blasé were sitting quietly by their pegs, reflecting on the event ahead.

One of the valets fastened on Melody Phipps's diamond stock-pin and tied the black-and-burgundy silk on to my hat. My fingers felt about as nimble as sausages, but it wasn't through fear now. It was due to the churning, tingling feel of anticipation and just wanting to get on. Outside, the buzz and rumble of thousands of excited spectators drifted in.

We were called outside for a group photograph. The goodwill and friendliness of everyone was unbelievable. All the jockeys were united by the same emotions.

Only Dougie Barnes kept his distance. As we gathered for the photograph, I was called into the centre of the first row and told to crouch down. I couldn't stop staring at the famous winner's enclosure, with its ornate flowers and cream-and-green decor and the overhang at the entrance. So many winning jockeys had had to duck quickly as their horse was led underneath, I wondered if it would be my turn today. I took it all in with the awe it deserved.

The briefing by the stewards was short and sharp. "Keep your heads. The going is as heavy as it gets. Take your time. No races to the first. Stay safe. Enjoy yourselves."

Frantically, I looked for Rory in the splash of jockeys' colours. We'd been drawn at opposite ends of the field. It would probably be the last time I'd see him to speak to until the race was over. At the final moment, before we set out to the paddock, I spotted his orange hoops.

"I love you," he mouthed.

"Me too." I grinned.

The parade down the side of the grandstands seemed to take for ever. The cheering was deafening and then a fanfare sounded on top of that. It was enough to rupture eardrums. Murphy high-stepped, super-charged and playing to the audience. I took my feet out of the stirrups to try to keep him relaxed, trick him into thinking we weren't going to race just yet. I stroked his steaming neck and spoke to him. Scooby was leading us, proudly striding out. Every hundred yards there was a fresh cheer from the crowds.

I felt a furry flake of snow on the tip of my nose. Then another. And another. It was snowing at Aintree. Everything was suddenly hushed, as if the whole place was holding its breath. Thick, soft snowflakes fell from the heavy sky until a blanket of white blotted out vision. Horses pranced sideways and jockeys ducked their heads. Murphy snorted into the cold air. Was this it? Was this how the dream would end? I closed my eyes in despair. There was no way they would run the race in weather like this.

Ten

"What's going on?" The jockey on the horse ahead had turned back down the line of runners but we were still being led towards the course. Nobody seemed to have a clue what to do. The steady snowfall muffled all sound.

Horses started sliding. Snow was balling up in their hooves, panicking them into skittering wrecks. What was usually a controlled, organized event turned into disarray. Scooby rested a hand on Murphy's neck, trying to calm him, but Murphy was psyched up to race. He didn't understand delays.

"They're turning us back!" A voice came from the front. "Turn around and head for the paddock!"

Was that it? Was the race abandoned, or just postponed? I sat tight as Murphy tried to half-rear and nearly lost his hindlegs. Scooby was holding on to his bridle for grim death. Up in the grandstands there was muted noise and confusion as people shuffled in and out of their seats. Nobody knew if there was going to be a race.

The procession of horses about turned and, with heads ducked between knees and tails clamped down, filed back into the parade paddock. There was a frantic rush from lads and trainers to throw rugs over vulnerable hind-quarters. It would be disastrous if these finely tuned animals got cold now. It was vital to keep them as warm as possible. I jumped off Murphy's back. Immediately, our team got to work.

The Guv'nor threw a waterproof jacket round my shoulders. "Go with the other jockeys. This isn't your place."

All I wanted to do was stay with Murphy and calm him.

The group of jockeys, hunched and deflated, headed back to the weighing room. A groan of disbelief and some foul language came from the front when the stewards wouldn't let us back in because we had been officially weighed out. The only alternative was to squash into the tent where the weighing scales were. At least it was under cover.

"They're bringing in helicopters to blow snow off the fences and away from the take off and landing areas." That was all the stewards seemed to know, but there was a definite lift of spirits.

All the jockeys wanted to carry on. They hadn't programmed themselves for anything else.

"Your horse ain't looking too good," Dougie Barnes leaned in close, a malicious smile on his face. I didn't wait to hear any more. I pushed through the huddle of bodies and went up to the verandah where I could look out over the parade ring.

A gasp from under the carpet of umbrellas by the ring sounded ominous. I looked in that direction. Murphy was plunging around, shaking his head and pawing wildly at the air. It was taking Scooby and Badger all their strength to hang on to him. I felt sick with despair and hopelessness. He was boiling over. He was winding himself up into a frenzy. He would be exhausted before we even began.

"There you are!" Rory came across to my side. "I've been looking for you everywhere." I couldn't move or speak. I was too busy watching all my efforts and dreams melt away into the snow.

Then suddenly, "It's stopping!"

A whoop went up from the jockeys. A glint of sunlight pushed through the grey mass of cloud. As quickly as it started, the snow stopped. The horses shook their manes and stepped out with easier strides.

After about half an hour we were told to

remount. The course was again rideable. Even the sun had come out.

Murphy wasn't right. I knew it as soon as he cantered down to warm up again and look at the first fence. He'd worn himself out with nerves – it had taken his edge.

Other horses blasted past, keen to be let off a tight rein. Jockeys pushed their mounts right up to the spruce fence, demanding they take a good look. Some shied, some tried to eat it, but very few realized they had to jump it. Murphy just stared disinterestedly. He had switched off. I could have cried.

Back at the start, the jockeys formed two large circles at walk. The anticipation was building. The banter died away. Each jockey was focusing on the race ahead. Nerves touched everyone.

A helicopter crossed overhead, ready to film from the air. I could see Rory raise his hand and mouth, "Good luck," but I was in a vacuum. It was just Murphy and the task ahead.

The starter called us forward. "Line up! Go on!" The horses shifted back and forth. I tightened my reins. A huge roar built up from the grandstand. The tape shot up. We were off.

Thirty-seven horses surged forward across Melling Road, the cinder track. The first jump was upon us. Some horses baulked with fear.

There was a faller on my right. A refusal to the left. Murphy climbed over but not with much daylight. His ears were back. The swish of hooves across the fence top was stunningly loud.

We were on to the next and the next. Every muscle and fibre in Murphy's body hated the going. He felt flat and depressed. We were surviving because he was picking his way through the fallers; he even twisted in mid-air to avoid one, but we were miles off the pace. For the first time in Murphy's racing career, he was at the tail end. We couldn't have been any further back.

I mentally vowed that if he hadn't improved by the Canal turn, we'd pull up. Compacted balls of slush and mud flew back like missiles from thundering hooves. I could hardly see. My goggles were clogged up. In desperation I pulled them down and fixed both hands back on the reins.

Bechers. A loose horse careered sideways not far from us. The noise from the crowds was tremendous. The ground sucked and popped as hooves plunged in. We started drifting off a straight line. Horses barged up on the right. We were boxed in. "Murphy – listen to me!" I screamed into his flattened ears. I started to talk to him, trying to spark his enthusiasm. It was our only chance to stay in the race. "Mind yourself. Go on a bit! Careful! There's a drop on the other side. Don't take off too close! Steady. Come back to me!"

It was working. The great red ears pricked up slightly. He changed legs and focused. Bechers hurtled towards us. Fence six. It looked as big as a forest. We took off alongside two other horses, drawing an arc through the air. Up, Up.

He cleared it! Other horses crashed through, but Murphy didn't touch a twig. "Steady! Steady! Steady!" The drop stretched on for ever. I let the reigns slide through my fingers, leaning back till I was nearly touching his tail. The jolt as we landed passed through his legs, right up through my body like an earth tremor. He was still upright! I grabbed at the reins and pulled him together. We were in one piece. We'd survived Bechers Brook, the Grand National's most infamous fence. I could feel the heady rush of adrenaline.

"Steady now, steady! Next, Foinavon, the famous seventh fence. We jumped clean. "It's the Canal Turn next, boy, you've got to jump on an angle. We can't afford to lose ground. You've got to twist in the air." The rush of speed whipped words out of my mouth but Murphy had a sixth sense. He knew what I wanted. I could feel him adjusting his stride.

Televison cars chased the leaders up ahead. We were two from the back. The ground was chewed up and the fences ravaged, but we could pick through like a cat. Belief had returned. We could do this. "Get ready Murphy; after three strides. Wait. Steady. Go! Go! Turn! Turn!"

We jack-knifed in mid-air. We couldn't have turned more tightly. Murphy found his feet and scorched away.

I had to make a decision. Should we pull up or keep going? If we kept going it would be an almighty test – we'd have to overtake the whole field. He'd lost so much energy before the race started. The ground was bog-like and dangerous.

"Tell me, Murphy. Tell me what to do!" I leaned in close to his neck, my face wet and mud-streaked. It was up to him. I needed a message, a sign.

He started to quicken. He dipped his head and grabbed hold of the bit. I could feel his determination rise up. He was making a conscious decision. He was running off with me. He was taking the race out of my hands. "Go on, Murphy, you can do it, you can. You're the best!"

He started to run. I sat quietly and locked into his rhythm. We picked off the other horses one by one. We were moving up the outside in a relentless, pounding gallop. We flew over Valentines, fence nine. On. On. Gaining ground. At the Chair, fence fifteen, a whole cluster of horses fell. I recognized Rory's orange hoops, but he was up on his

116

feet, unharmed. "Go on, Murphy, go!" He yelled encouragement.

We were flying. The water loomed up. Fence sixteen. Murphy soared over it, splaying his legs and overtaking two horses in mid-air. There was an almighty roar as we passed the grandstand. Murphy heard and it lifted him. As we set out over Melling Road for the final time, half the field had dropped out of the race. There were nine horses ahead in a bunch. The Black was further on, in the lead.

We had it all to do. The Guv'nor's face blurred in front of me. "Assess the situation. Think fast. Work out your strategy," he had said. It was my turn to take charge of the race again. I had to ride as I had never ridden before.

As we caught up with the group ahead I tried to gauge who had petrol left in the tank. Banjo Boy looked as if he was about spent. Two horses on my left dropped away, exhausted. It was hard to judge the rest but The Black was still going strong and drawing further away.

We came down to Bechers for the second time. The course was scattered with spruce. Two holes to the outside of the fence were obvious places to jump. Murphy popped over, annoyed that he was cheated of a massive jump. His spirit was soaring. Every time we overtook a horse he flashed his ears back and lengthened his stride. He was enjoying every minute.

I lined him up for the Canal Turn for the second time and could have sworn he remembered the lessons the Guv had given us back at Dolphin. He jumped it brilliantly. Valentines. Fence twenty-eight. Melling Road. Three horses left. We surged on. Exhaustion made me weak in the saddle. I had to grasp a handful of mane. Despite every effort, my body was floppy and I felt disorientated. I don't think I'd drawn breath since Bechers, first time round.

We landed over the Chair for the final time and suddenly there was nobody in front of us but The Black. We were drawing level with the television car. We were plastered with mud, as if someone had attacked us with a spray gun. My goggles dangled under my chin and I'd lost the silk off my hat. But still Murphy went forward, clearing the water jump with ease. He had one target and he was chasing it, for all he was worth.

Suddenly we were racing to the Liverpool elbow, the point where the running rail bends to funnel the racers to the winning post. It was a long haul, another race in itself, and The Black was still a good ten lengths ahead. The noise from the grandstand was awesome. Every person there must have been on their feet, shouting at the tops of their lungs. Murphy wobbled and hesitated. He was spent. He couldn't respond to the applause of his fans. He'd given his all.

"It's OK, boy, well done." I patted his neck over and over. He'd done miraculously. I was bursting with pride. We'd come second and that was an amazing achievement for what people had called a scrap-heap horse and a slip of a girl.

Still the crowds yelled and screamed. I saw The Black ahead falter and drift. Dougie Barnes glanced round and grinned when he saw we weren't a threat. The winning post was in sight. I let my reins go loose. There was no way I'd ask more of Murphy. He'd given his soul. He was the people's champion and they loved his courage. I put my head down and prepared to canter to the line.

Suddenly Murphy took hold of the bit again. He surged forward, gaining valuable lengths. The crowd went crazy. He lowered his head and plunged for the line. With disbelief I saw the gap close. The Black was finished. He had nothing else to give. He was hanging on by a thread. And Murphy was determined. He'd got his second wind. The sound from the grandstand was incredible. Murphy responded in one last, courageous effort. We drew level with The Black's shoulder. I saw the panic on Barnes's face as Murphy stretched out his neck. I focused on the winning post. Murphy had won the Grand National!

I collapsed over Murphy's neck. I couldn't fall off, not now. I clung to his mane and saw the police horses move in, one on each side. I was in shock. Murphy had to find his own way off the course. Exhaustion and elation swirled through me. The cheering went on. People were crying and laughing, hugging each other and shouting. Everyone was aware of what we'd done but me. Murphy had shown courage beyond belief. The whole country was responding to it in heartfelt delight. And suddenly it hit me. We'd done it. We'd won.

Murphy stepped into the chaotic throng without a moment's hesitation. His ears flicked back and forth, soaking up the adoration. Everyone wanted to touch him, to reach out to the great red horse.

I felt as weak as a kitten, crying and laughing but somehow managing to cling on to the tiny saddle. Then I saw Rory pushing through the crowd. I wanted him right by me. Thunderous applause burst out and I ducked my head as we were led into the famous winners' enclosure. I registered Scooby, crying like a baby with his arms round Murphy's neck. And the Guv'nor, tearful and moved beyond words. Together we'd achieved the impossible. My parents were pushing through the crowd towards me, tears in their eyes. Reporters rushed forward with microphones. I slid from the saddle and clung to Murphy's shoulder, I needed a minute, needed desperately to thank him for his incredible strength and courage. Together we had made history, fulfilled a dream. But above all, he was the people's champion and for the rest of his days he would be an inspiration.

I felt a familiar hand on my shoulder then. A mud-spattered cheek and lips on the side of my face. Rory swung me round and threw his arms round my shaking body. That was all I needed to know it was real, it had really happened. I kissed him with a love I knew would last for ever and felt him lift me right off my feet.

"You've done it, Jus! You've won the Grand National! You're a true champion!"

I was and so was my horse, the brilliant Murphy's Law.

Glossary

box walker – A horse which paces around its stable endlessly, fretting and wearing itself out.

chaps – Usually made of leather, they are worn over trousers as protection against dirt while riding.

filling – Swelling.

first/second lot – The first and second work rides of the day.

furlong – An eighth of a mile.

guinea – The equivalent of £1.05.

racing plate – A lightweight horseshoe which horses wear for racing.

seller – Also called a claims race, where the horses can be bought for a set price after the race.

steeplechase – A horse race with a set number of obstacles including a water jump. Originally a cross-country race from town steeple to town steeple.

surcingle – A belt or strap used to keep a day or night rug in position.
upsides – Riding alongside another horse.